MEDDLING HEROES

BY CHARLIE BROOKS

Copyright © 2023 Charlie Brooks. All rights reserved.
ISBN: 978-0-578-87033-5

For Quentin and Cordelia

#1: THE MOST DANGEROUS MAN ON EARTH

Every day, my captors wake me up, strip me naked, and check for microchips in my brain.

This morning, three armed guards stand on the far end of the corridor facing my cell. Dressed in riot gear, they keep assault rifles trained on me as I remove my clothes. Two more guards stand in front of the locked door, pistols ready.

I count four regulars and one rookie on mad scientist detail today. The new kid hangs in back, keeping his finger on the trigger and ignoring proper gun safety. New blood makes my mornings more exciting, but also increases my odds of catching a bullet if I unbutton my fly too quickly. Fear makes people do stupid things.

I didn't earn nine PhDs and shrink the state of Delaware to pocket size just so I could die in prison because somebody thinks the naked super-genius wants to take over the world from his cell. I just want some toast and oatmeal.

I fold my gray uniform neatly and place the clothes precisely two feet from the cell door. Then I step back and sit on the edge of my bed with my hands up and my feet flat on the floor. One of the door guards opens my cell, and the other scrambles forward to put the clothing in a clear plastic bag. She then places a new uniform down and steps back into the hallway, never taking his eyes off me.

Mornings used to feel awkward, but I've stopped being self-conscious about my nudity. After 1,829 days of this routine, I don't have much choice but to accept it.

From my understanding, the bagged uniform goes to a group of forensic scientists who examine my clothes under a black light and a microscope, light it on fire, mix the ashes with concrete, and ship the remains to a landfill in the Arizona desert. In the early days of my incarceration, I may or may not have made a couple idle threats that gave certain people the impression that a hidden satellite in orbit around the planet can home in on any trace of my DNA.

Despite occasional lapses like that one, I usually have the good sense to stay quiet. True, I did slightly threaten death on eight of the nine sitting Supreme Court Justices when they rejected my appeal, but everybody has days like that. I just hope my lawyer can successfully spin my diatribe as a moment of stress-induced insanity rather than a legitimate plan to show those fools and meddling heroes what a true genius can do.

Once I have new clothes on, I turn around and place my hands behind my back so one of the guards can handcuff me. The other passes an electric wand across my head and body, ensuring that I haven't hidden any foreign objects on my person in the last twenty-four hours.

I catch a little bit of my reflection in the chrome of the scanner and muse that my already short hair has begun thinning recently. In my prime, I could crash the Earth's moon into Jupiter, but I never figured out a long-term cure for male pattern baldness.

"You're clean again today," the scan-man says as he takes his equipment out of the cell.

"Just like every day," I respond. My voice sounds raspy from lack of use. "Has the warden still not realized I know the specifications of those scanners? If I wanted to hide something, I'd do it in a way you'd never pick up."

"Of course, of course," says the guard who handcuffed me. "One day, you'll show us all, right?"

I swallow my pride and just grin as the others guffaw in my direction. I wait until they uncuff me and leave before I allow myself the satisfaction of a response.

"No," I mutter. "It's too late for me to show you. You'll have to learn the hard way now."

I really should avoid saying such things, even when I'm alone. Sometimes, though, I just can't help myself. I never monologued much when I was in action. Now that I've spent the last five years in prison, I feel like I have a lot to make up for.

A supervillain who talks too much can take some solace in thinking he beat himself. All through my last days of freedom, I kept my mouth shut. When Paradigm and Miss Destiny tore through my hidden lair, I didn't explain to them that their power was useless against my titanium battle suit. And so instead of looking back and thinking, "If only I had shut up, I could have won," I have to face the hard truth as to why I'm here: I just got beat.

I didn't count on the time-traveling Captain Tomorrow jumping two weeks into the past and placing a fatal flaw in my battle suit. I didn't count on Paradigm cracking the helmet open and nearly splitting my billion-dollar brain in the process. I was the smartest man in the world, and that made me the most dangerous man on Earth. I had plans on top of plans. I figured no one could beat me but myself.

Unfortunately, plans only keep someone going until someone punches him in the face.

They emptied the entire cellblock after my first month here. Somebody saw my skinny 5'5" frame and figured they could get a reputation boost from taking out the man who single-handedly broke up the League of Liberty. The big man ignored the fact that I had spent the better part of a decade fighting superheroes. Even if you rely on your brain, you need some martial arts training—certainly enough to break a thug's kneecaps when he tries to shiv you from behind. They've left me alone since then, leaving me surrounded by laser-guided surveillance equipment and state-of-the art weaponry capable of turning me into lead-filled hamburger should I ever step outside my cell without permission.

They leave me alone with my dreams for four hours after breakfast. At noon, the same small battalion that watched me dress this morning arrives to give me something special.

"You know the drill," the leader says while the others train guns on me. "It's time to take a walk."

I nod and lie face down on the floor, hands behind me so they can cuff me again. Once my wrists are secure, the guard hauls me back onto my feet and leads me out of the cell. I hear the electric crackle of a stun gun behind me, ready to shut down my nervous system at the slightest provocation.

"Just so you know, I could have escaped anytime I wanted," I tell my escorts.

The guard behind me laughs. "Whatever you say, Doc."

The sound of her laughter makes my blood boil in a way that no other insult could. I grit my teeth as we move, contemplating all the ways I could show them the truth. With a nickel and some wire, I could override their paltry little security system and turn the entire prison into a fortress that obeys me as a master. Even now, the woman with the stun gun thinks she has the advantage, but I could stop in my tracks, lunge backwards, and knock her down while I grab her keys. Before anyone else could react, I'd be free of my cuffs and using the toy soldier as a meat shield. Not the most elegant plan, but I'd give myself 50/50 odds of winning such a fight. I can be the nicest man in the world, as long as you don't laugh at me.

But no…I take a deep breath and let the guards push me through the copper and urine stench of this prison as if I'm some lost calf. I'm beyond the need for petty revenge now. I got beat, and I'm not about to be a sore loser. Besides, today is my day in court.

For a long while, I hear only the sound of footsteps from my soft-soled slippers contrasting with the combat boots worn by my escorts. But eventually, I hear something precious: the sound of other people.

Other prisoners, ones with more rights and privileges, ones that didn't build a functioning space station at the age of eighteen, lounge in a common room, talking and laughing as a television behind a mesh cage plays the news. It's a reminder that there's a world outside my cell. Very soon, that will be my world again.

I take a chance and stop to glance at the TV. The anchors in the safe haven of their newsroom speak with a brown-haired woman on the streets. It takes me a moment to place the woman's face—she's gained wrinkles and a few gray hairs since I last saw her. Then I smile as I remember. Good old Betsy Bryant, that nosey reporter. I guess the world hasn't changed that much after all. We're all a little older, but planet Earth is still familiar to me.

"Police have released only a few details of the investigation, but they did indicate that the victim was none other than the time-traveling vigilante known as Captain Tomorrow."

Very nice wording, my dear: "they did indicate." It sounds better on television than, "I twisted their arms and browbeat them into leaking some information."

"There was another apparent victim whose presence remains completely unexplained," Betsy continues. "Police found the body of the notorious Dr. Roosevelt Pythagoras at the scene. How this is possible, considering that Dr. Pythagoras is still being held in federal custody, has most of the scientific community baffled."

That name…my name. The first time I've heard anyone say my full name in almost half a decade, and it comes from that infuriating woman. How splendid.

In the common room, the other prisoners turn their heads in unison to stare at me. I see the puzzlement and the fear on their faces, and I love it. They want to know the same thing everyone else is wondering: how can I be dead in an alley and standing in front of them at the same time?

The shared slack-jawed expression thrills me the most: the sheer wonder of an untrained human brain trying to explain the impossible. Captain Tomorrow is dead, and so am I. But I'm also here in prison. And that is my key out of this place.

Most of all, I relish the sound of my name spoken on television. Roosevelt Pythagoras…the man who doesn't need a secret identity. If I hadn't had my revelation during my stay in prison,

I'd be laughing now. A long, loud, maniacal laugh, the kind that only the truly brilliant can appreciate.

"Get moving," the guard behind me says, shoving me forward and putting me back on my path to freedom.

I let the indignity slide. I am Roosevelt Pythagoras, and today is my day in court.

#2: SPEAKING FOR THE DEFENSE

My name is Eva Corson. Over the years, I've represented sentient robots, hyper-intelligent gorillas, and time-displaced cavemen. They all followed one simple rule: they wore pants in my office.

Leave it to Paradigm, the supposed symbol of America, to break that rule. I don't care if the people on the news call it a uniform; he's wearing red tights with blue underwear on the outside, and he's doing it in my workplace.

He thinks that meeting with me in person can put me off-balance. Instead, I fold my hands and let my office speak for me. The shelves of legal books and certificates speak to my education. The pictures of some of Paradigm's greatest enemies shaking my hand as they walk free speaks to his grudge against me.

"Eva, you can't follow through with this case," he declares.

"Oh, it's Eva now, is it?" I retort." "Not Miss Corson? Not the dozen or so curses you're probably thinking of right now?"

"I don't watch violent television. I doubt I'd even know the words you're imagining me thinking."

I suddenly wish I had a pair of glasses so I could look sternly over the top of my frames at him. In person, he's the same type of pretty boy do-gooder I see on billboards telling kids to eat their breakfast and get lots of exercise. I despise anyone who seems that perfect. It makes me wonder what might happen if they finally did crack.

"Anyway," he continues in his stern but calm voice, "you can read whatever you want into my words. The important thing is that you hear me out."

According to the government's superhero database, Paradigm stands 6'3". He looks taller in person, with his ridiculous spandex outfit seeming to exist for no reason except to display the muscles on his perfect physique. I find it endlessly ironic that the man who saved the world from the Nazis is a blond-haired, blue-eyed, eternally young superman.

Reading Paradigm's face is nearly impossible, and not just because of the powder blue mask covering most of it. He looks like he's carved out of stone, leaving me to scan for minor twitches and almost imperceptible changes in body language to figure out what's going on in his skull.

"You must have heard by now that somebody murdered one of my people," he says. "They found a body genetically identical to Pythagoras nearby."

"I know that perfectly well," I retort. "In fact, it's a key part of this case."

"If you win, Captain Tomorrow won't be the only superhero found dead in the streets," he snaps back.

"You're not seriously implying that my client is responsible for his death? He was sitting in prison the whole time."

"You're trying to apply normal logic to an abnormal situation, Miss Corson." He doesn't realize it, but he's using the same patronizing tone a teacher would reserve for a misbehaving grade schooler. "Whatever cage they threw him in, Pythagoras still has more anti-super technology hidden away than anyone else on the planet."

"Allegedly."

"Excuse my language, but I still have scars from that darned titanium death-bot of his."

I cock an eyebrow for a couple reasons. First, I realize that "darned" is apparently a curse word to him. Second, the lewder part of my mind wonders where those scars are.

I check my watch and stand up. I'm a tall woman—not as tall as the walking tank here, but close enough to let him know I won't be intimidated. Tilting my head slightly upward, I look him in the eyes as I speak.

"Through four appeals, you never batted an eye. Now suddenly the evidence lines up to match my client's alibi, and you show up in my office begging me to violate everything I stand for and drop the case. If you have as much faith in America as you say you do in your damned PSAs, you'll let the courts decide innocence or guilt."

He tenses slightly. The white star on his chest expands a little and then returns to normal as he works to control his breathing. He can shrug off anything short of a direct hit with a missile, but I still know how to throw jabs that hurt.

"You know I trust the system," he growls.

"If you did, you wouldn't be here," I snap. "And you wouldn't be referring to a dead vigilante as one of 'your people.' You know what they say about 'my people?' Five hundred at the bottom of the ocean is a good start."

"You make your living defending supervillains, Miss Corson."

"I make my living defending *people*," I correct. "And unless you feel like overthrowing the government, they get the same rights as you do. I'm not about to keep my client behind bars because someone who fights giant monsters and alien assassins couldn't beat the odds one more time."

He folds his arms and glares at me for a long time. "Fine," he finally says. "Do your job, and I'll do mine. But I'll be keeping an eye on him...and you."

He turns and walks away, his blue cape billowing outward in a dramatic flutter. I'm just glad he didn't fly through my wall out of spite.

"Fine," I say, collecting my notes for the appeal. "Just for a change, though, try going through the cops like everybody else."

Police can get quite punctual when transporting a man who knows how to build a nuclear bomb from memory. Running late thanks to my argument with Paradigm, I meet up with my client at the courthouse. He sits on the sofa in the defendant's lobby, drinking tea from a foam cup. He wears in a black shirt and blazer, a white tie, and brown leather shoes an outfit he calls his power suit. As he once pointed out to me, the power suit is different from the battle suit, which involves booster jets and anti-tank weaponry.

"It still fits," he says, setting his tea down and standing up to greet me as I enter the lobby. "Tassels on the shoes are still the style, aren't they?"

"They were never the style, Rosey," I inform him.

His face falls. I think deep down Roosevelt Pythagoras always wanted to be a villain out of some superspy movie, complete with a fluffy white cat to stroke menacingly and a big collection of witty one-liners. But that's just not the world we live in. Superheroes forced his hand.

"Do you really think we're going to get through this time?" he asks, his eyes a bit wider and more childlike than he probably wants them to be.

"You remember what to say when I put you on the stand?" I ask.

"I've had it memorized for years now," he responds.

"Then yes, you'll be a free man by the end of today."

"What makes you so sure this appeal will work when all the others have failed?"

"This isn't just an appeal of the sentence, or potential bias in the court," I explain. "This is basically a whole new trial. We finally have some proof to back up the alibi you stuck to for five years. A superhero just died, and the man who might be able to figure out how and why has been wrongly imprisoned. The people are afraid of the system failing, and that gives us an edge we didn't have before. They even granted you a bond to be here; that's proof that things are different this time."

"And the fact that neither of us know where this 'clone' of mine came from doesn't bother you?"

"We play the hand we're dealt. You promised me you'd figure this out, and I that's good enough for me."

"If that deal you told me about comes through, I'll find the truth. But I still don't understand how you got her to—"

"Relax," I interrupt. "It's going to work."

He pulls a loose thread away from his cuff and tosses it aside. "Don't think I don't trust you," he sniffs, a little upset that I understand something he doesn't. "But how can you be so sure? Evidence is all well and good, but people are...people." His mouth tightens and his eyes narrow. "People are variables you can't account for."

"Let's put it this way...Paradigm thinks you're going to go free."

His eyes light up like I just read off the entire periodic table of elements from memory. "You talked to Paradigm?"

I nod. "He showed up in my office not more than an hour ago."

"What did he want?"

"He practically begged me to drop your case. He knows you're about to hit the streets again."

He double checks to make sure the door and windows are closed. "We have complete privacy here?"

"Attorney-client privilege. The chambers are practically soundproof."

"Do you mind?"

"No...go right ahead."

"Heh...heh heh...heh heh heh heh..." His laughter begins slowly, as though he's trying to remember how to let it out. Then it spills forth, a flood of madness and joy from his mouth. Every horror movie he watched as a child, every genius with a grudge he idolized growing up has taught him that the only way the truly brilliant let out their mirth is through loud, maniacal laughter. By now, he's so set in his ways that I'm not going to be the one to change him.

"Heh...sorry about that," he concludes, wiping a tear from his eye. "It's been a long time."

"Don't worry about it," I say reassuringly. "You'd be surprised at how often I get that out of my clients."

He'd probably also be surprised at how many repeat clients I have, but he doesn't need to know that.

"You know, it occurs to me that after this is all over, I won't have much of a chance to let loose like that again."

"If you do, just make sure you do it in the privacy of your own home."

He glances at his tasseled shoes and then looks back up toward my face. "I'm going to need someone to assist me when I get out," he says. "Preferably someone with legal knowhow."

"I do happen to have a practice of my own, you know."

"It wouldn't interfere with that...it would be more like putting you on retainer. Helping me out a bit in my new career."

"Do you think you can afford me?"

He gives me a sloppy, confident grin. "My dear, you'd be surprised at the assets I still possess." He offers me his arm like he's ushering me into a wedding. "Shall we?"

"Yes, we shall."

I take his arm and escort my prize client toward the courtroom. In just a little while, the most successful supervillain in history will walk out of here a free man.

#3: THOSE THRILLING DAYS OF YESTERYEAR

I designed my battle suit to survive a nuclear explosion at ground zero, so you can imagine my surprise when bare fists cracked it open. Even though those fists belonged to Paradigm, the nuclear man, it took me by surprise. I have never handled surprise well.

"That—that's not possible!" I shrieked as the titanium helmet buckled under the force of the blow. Those were the first words I had spoken during the entire battle—I knew anything I said would get picked up by my own security systems, and I didn't want to let anything slip that might be used against me later.

Not that I expected to lose, mind you. Even with my plans to harness control of the Earth's magnetic field revealed, I always thought I was going to come out of this battle a winner. But one must be prepared.

Paradigm's slender fingers dug into the side of my helmet, sinking into the metal as though it were putty. I always assumed he'd have rough, blistered hands from his years as a soldier or maybe his time as a farmer before then. Instead he had smooth skin with perfectly trimmed nails, like he spent his days playing piano instead of flying through the sun.

"You're finished, Pythagoras," he said authoritatively as he tore the helmet away, revealing my face to the cameras.

"That can't happen! My calculations were perfect!"

Paradigm didn't respond—he put all his effort into tearing my battle suit to shreds. The plutonium-tipped blades had done a number on him, leaving him with deep gashes across his chest and arms. He took the damage personally, not stopping until he had completely ripped away the suit and destroyed my ability to ever challenge his power again.

It's a shame he had to be so destructive. The suit was what passed for stylish in the heroing world—chromed silver everywhere and retractable blades that seemed to defy the laws of physics. Had Paradigm been less thorough, fashion designers could have had a field day with it. Instead, all the cameras got to see at the end of the fight was a sweaty genius wearing nothing but a pair of briefs. Paradigm folded his arms and hovered a few feet above me, his tattered cape still flowing majestically behind him. Maybe it was just the concussion talking, but I swear I could hear theme music somewhere.

"It must have taken you months to build that suit," came a familiar middle-aged voice. I heard footsteps behind Paradigm, and another man came into view. He wore a brown trench coat and hooded cowl, with a pair of aviator-style goggles over his eyes. "Armor thick enough to absorb our best hits, blades sharp enough to kill. Too bad you can't fight time."

"What...is that your catch phrase now?" I asked.

Captain Tomorrow ignored me and focused on his own companions. "Are you all right, Miss Destiny?"

"Yes," responded the woman I had previously tossed through a wall. She wore a blue and gold jumpsuit and a cape with a flared collar. Even in the dim light of my lair, the gold medallion around her neck shined brightly. "A few broken bones, but I will heal while our foe is in jail."

"Miss Destiny destroyed your tachyon interferers while Paradigm kept you busy," Captain Tomorrow explained. "Then I jumped a couple of weeks back and putting a small but fatal flaw in your armor..."

If I have any regrets about the way I went down, it boils down to the fact that I didn't rig up my teleporter as a last-ditch contingency. For all the ridicule criminals get for their wicked diatribes, the crime fighters talk just as much. I probably could have escaped if I had counted on the post-fight monologues. Then again, with no lair or equipment, my battle suit torn to shreds, and my assets frozen by the government for crimes against humanity, I don't know how far I would have made it.

"...Paradigm did the rest, and now we've finally got you," said Captain Tomorrow, ending a speech that I had tuned out about halfway through.

"Curses," is all I managed to say. I didn't speak again until my trial.

The surveillance video retrieved from my volcanic lair cuts out there. The District Attorney, a thin man with gold-rimmed glasses who breathes entirely too loudly through his nostrils, takes a few moments of silence to allow the panel of judges to digest what they saw. Then he smooths out his gray suit and resumes his questioning of me.

"Now, Dr. Pythagoras," he asks with an air of unearned smugness, "do you deny that the person in that video is you?"

"Considering that I got turned over to police custody immediately, I don't think it would make any sense for me to deny it," I reply matter-of-factly.

"You have claimed time and again that your crimes were committed by somebody else," he continues, "and yet now you openly admit that the man in that footage is you."

"Yes, but—"

"That's enough." He smiles confidently and returns to the bench. "No further questions."

I tap my finger impatiently on the witness stand, waiting to have my say. Almost as if to tease me, Eva takes her time preparing her notes. Despite my impatience, she becomes a calming influence once she stands up, taking measured steps and wearing a confident smile. Her face is thin and dark, and she doesn't have a single hair out of place. She's like me—she has a plan for almost everything. The difference is that where I know machines, she knows people. That's why I need her for Phase Two.

"Dr. Pythagoras," she practically purrs at me as she says my name. "Could you tell the court what crimes you saw committed in that surveillance video?"

"Considering I had legally purchased the island where the fight took place and I owned all the equipment I used in my experiments, the only crime I see committed is an intrusion on private property," I respond.

"Your home defense systems included a rocket-proof battle suit and razor-sharp retractable blades?" she asks, as if she doesn't already know the answer.

"Considering my opponent, I though it appropriate."

"And who was your opponent?"

"Myself, of course."

"Objection!" shouts the DA.

One of the judges furrows his bushy white eyebrows together and glares at Eva, waiting for an explanation.

Eva smiles and answers the challenge. "I'm reviewing important history behind this battle. Moreover, I'm establishing that, given the new evidence that has been presented, the supposed crimes committed here are a series of errors, all led by a severe case of mistaken identity."

"Proceed," orders the judge.

Eva nods and resumes her questioning. "Dr. Pythagoras, perhaps you could give us the background of these events from your perspective?"

"I'd love to, but it goes quite a number of years back."

"Please, tell us whatever facts you deem relevant." Eva purses her burgundy lips at me, like this is a game to her. Maybe it is, and that thought just makes me happier to have her playing on my side.

"Well, approximately twelve years ago, I began a research project on human cloning with my company, RP Industries. Because of the risks involved, I became the first test subject."

"Isn't the founder of a multinational corporation experimenting on himself a little unorthodox?"

"It is, but so was this experiment. Normal cloning projects create a genetic duplicate from birth and let that new life grow normally. This one involved artificially aging the clone and implanting my own memories in it, essentially making an exact copy of an existing person. The project built upon my own independent research. It had numerous potential dangers, and I didn't want to put anyone else at risk. Looking back, I probably shouldn't have undertaken it at all."

"And why do you say that?"

"The clone escaped the test facility after going totally insane. Disguised as me, he proceeded to embezzle funds from my company to support his own independent research. After a particularly br—"

Eva draws her index finger across her throat, warning me not to say "brilliant."

"...brazen plan that could have destroyed the world, I decided to take matters into my own hands. Most of the world thought me responsible by this time, and the board of directors ousted me as head of my own company. Luckily, I had previously purchased an isolated island to serve as my private getaway. I prepared for the fight of my life there, but the three 'heroes' broke in and attacked me before I could explain myself."

"But...a battle suit? A magma-powered energy reactor? A small army of androids? Were these really necessary to defeat one man?"

"I know my capabilities," I answer. "If I could build all those things, so could my clone. And because of his mental defect, he was more dangerous than me, seeking to destroy humanity instead of help it. He was capable of anything, and the authorities would have arrested me on sight had I approached them for help. One might argue that I shouldn't have taken matters into my own hands, but it's not like the past few decades haven't provided a certain...precedent for vigilante justice."

"This is the story you've maintained for five years—that your clone committed the crimes you were blamed for."

"It's the truth. Unfortunately, the clone himself went into hiding after my defeat. He probably realized how close he came to winding up in my place and decided to regroup and come up with a new plan."

"And again, the state questions the relevance of any of this testimony," the DA chimes in. "We're retreading territory already discussed in Dr. Pythagoras' original conviction."

"Up until recently, the story seemed ludicrous, even in the strange world we live in," Eva explains. "Until Captain Tomorrow's recent death, that is. Police found a body genetically identical to my client at the scene. But, as my client is alive and well on the stand right now, the explanation of a missing clone suddenly becomes more than just a flimsy excuse."

The DA glowers. "Captain Tomorrow traveled time. He could just as easily have pulled Dr. Pythagoras along with him."

Eva shakes her head. "We have the benefit of extensive documentation on the use of Captain Tomorrow's technology, courtesy of both his time with the League of Liberty and his close work with the federal government after they disbanded. Every record available indicates that his technology could only transport one person forward or backward in time."

"And you're defending one of the only people on the planet capable of modifying those tools," says an increasingly irritated DA.

Eva takes the verbal jab on the chin without flinching. "How would my client do that? He has no money, no lab, no resources to speak of. Unless he got assistance from Captain Tomorrow himself, it would take years to unravel this technology—and the body the police recovered has no notable age difference to Roosevelt Pythagoras today."

The head judge bangs his gavel, bringing an end to the oral melee. "Let the evidence speak for itself," he says wearily, "and get to the point, Ms. Corson."

"Happily," replies Eva. "We can speculate for weeks about the death of Captain Tomorrow and the body they found next to him. None of us know yet what happened, but we cannot deny the nature of the body as genetically identical to my client. Five years ago, a jury declared Dr. Pythagoras guilty because his alibi seemed too unbelievable to accept. But now we have something that makes his story possible. So the court must decide: can we as a society be sure beyond the shadow of a doubt that we have not taken five years of life away from an innocent man?"

Eva's voice rises as the buzz of discussion spreads through the court's audience. She's planted the seeds of doubt, and she knows exactly how well they'll grow. While the judges try to restore order, my eyes scan the crowd. Standing behind the bailiffs and wearing a press pass is a blond man with thick glasses and a convincing but definitely fake mustache. He's always avoided getting this close to me in this identity, because a mask only hides so much. This time, though, our eyes meet, and I smile.

They process my release remarkably quickly; I'm a free man in less than 48 hours. Once I get through the paperwork and lose the press, I head for the tallest building I can find. The evening air is crisp and the lights of the skyline look like a million sparkling gemstones. I hop up and down experimentally, testing my muscles. I walked the yard in isolation at the prison, but I never got the blood really pumping. The only part of me that's remained active is my mind. Fortunately, that's the important part.

I don't see him approach—his dark red and blue costume makes him hard to pinpoint in the nighttime sky. It doesn't surprise me, though, when I hear his voice behind me. We both knew he'd be the first person I'd hear from as a free man.

"I'll expose your lies eventually." Paradigm's voice has an unfamiliar fatigue to it. "The next time you slip up, I'll make sure you don't get a chance at an appeal."

I crouch and rub my hand across the rooftop. The concrete surface is rough—a consistency I never felt in prison, with its smooth walls and lack of debris that I might use for my own ends. Paradigm clears his throat, and I turn around, a dreamy smile on my face. He doesn't seem amused.

"You think you've won, but you'll have even less freedom than before," he warns. "Every cape and mask in this city is going to keep their attention focused on you, Pythagoras."

"That would be a terrible waste of time. I'm not totally free, you know. I have to check in every few hours with the authorities. I need to wear a GPS tracking device for at least thirty days. Let the real police do their job. You have muggers and monsters to fight, don't you?"

He doesn't land; he always floats a few feet above me, looking down on me. Looking down on all humanity, for all I can see.

"You're not as smart as you think you are," he growls. "I know that clone story of yours isn't true."

"Then how do you explain that other me the police found?"

"I'll figure you out. I always do."

"It should be easy, then. We'll be seeing more of each other than ever before."

A twitch of an eye tells me I know something he doesn't. "What are you talking about?"

"Why do you think Eva was able to swing this? Even with her legal clout, we needed something to assure the public I could put my mind to good use. Thanks to a few deals she's made, I'll be serving as a consultant on the investigation of Captain Tomorrow's death."

Every muscle tenses. His chin and cheeks become almost as red as his costume.

"You're bluffing. No one will let you within five miles of a crime scene."

"Oh, I'm sure whatever access they give me will be plenty. My analytical ability didn't just disappear while I was in jail, you know. Muscles get weak, but the brain remains strong. There's just one small stipulation."

"What's that?"

"Supervision, of course. They want a hero standing by in case I go rogue. You'll be getting a message from Eva soon enough—we'd like you to be the one to watch me."

He makes a fist, and for a moment I worry that he's going to knock the building down. But no—he's still in control for now. A nuclear reactor simmering away but never quite melting down.

"Why me?" he asks.

"Because nobody trusts me less than you do. If you're on board watching me with those super-eyes of yours and ready to twist my head off the moment I step out of line, then that cuts down on everybody else's fears of me trying to take over the world."

"Forget it," he snaps. "Everybody else in this sick little city might be willing to play your games, but I won't. I've got better things to do than babysit a madman like you."

I sigh a half-second too soon, possibly tipping him off to the fact that I've rehearsed this conversation in a mirror. "I told Eva you wouldn't be interested. She'll probably call you anyway. Protocol and all that. Doesn't matter, really. My B option has already accepted."

"Your 'B option?'"

"Of course. I have a backup plan for everything. Miss Destiny doesn't have quite the level of regard you do, but she can keep those marvelous spells of hers trained on me at all times. It didn't even take a rooftop conversation to get that deal done—Eva had it prepared before they finished processing my release. You see, Paradigm, everybody else is willing to play along and give me my second chance. The only one being overly paranoid about all this is you."

"I'm not paranoid. I'm prepared."

His words sound like an echo from my past. I repeated that sentiment to anybody who ever questioned my grudge against Paradigm. I didn't have time to hope for the best because I was always busy preparing for the worst. Now he has a taste of how I felt. I wonder if I'll ever get to see the world through his eyes.

I shouldn't keep prodding him, but I can't help myself. "Don't be so concerned," I say. "I'm just following the example you set. Even if we're just ordinary citizens, we can always put on a new mask and help fight crime, can't we?"

Somewhere in that dim bulb brain of his, he realizes he can't intimidate me here. Rather than stick around and let me keep the upper hand, he rockets away into the sky. I step backwards and squint my eyes at the sudden rush of warm air that follows him in flight, like afterburners on a jet. But he's not running as hot as he used to.

In fact, you're not the man you used to be at all, are you Paradigm? That skintight suit isn't quite as flattering as it once was, and your face has a few wrinkles that weren't there before.

You're getting old, while I feel younger than ever.

#4: THE SECRET LIFE OF A SUPERHERO

*E*instein told the President to make a bomb. Instead, they made a man.

Some people maintain that superheroes existed before the Nazis forced our hand. They believe that mythical figures such as Merlin and Samson were real, or that the Greek gods were ancestors of the modern-day superhero. Whatever old legends might have a grain of truth, the idea of an atomic bomb shaped the world as Rosey and I know it.

The details of what disaster ended the Manhattan Project remain classified by the United States government to this day. All anybody knows for sure is that some sort of accident during a test of the bomb created a nuclear man—the American Paradigm. He tore apart two Japanese cities single-handedly. To this day, Japan still doesn't allow superheroes to operate within its borders. The idea of a flying man terrifies that entire nation.

In some alternate universe, maybe the Manhattan Project went according to plan. Maybe someone's mistake didn't irradiate a soldier and turn him into an atomic superman. And maybe those who watched the old war documentaries didn't start to wonder what exactly might happen if Paradigm ever went rogue.

That's the only explanation I can think of for Rosey—he's afraid of what superheroes could do if they forgot the "hero" part of the word. A young Roosevelt Pythagoras, picked on in school, ridiculed for his puny stature, watched a video of the perfect man in action. I have to assume Rosey saw Paradigm as the ultimate bully—physically perfect and given a license by the American people to think with his fists.

I can't say Rosey's right. If Paradigm were going to snap, he surely would have done it decades ago. But I also don't accept the idea that Paradigm is entirely good, and I refuse to believe that Rosey is as mad as people say. If I'm wrong, it means I've made a huge mistake in setting him free.

Now Rosey stands in the home of a man that not even Paradigm's might could save. Two full SWAT divisions surround the house. A lieutenant and a detective lean against the wall as Rosey snoops around. Miss Destiny stands in stoic observation, hands clasped behind her back and watching his every move.

"Is my client really going to go through this entire investigation with cops dogging his every footstep?" I ask Miss Destiny.

She turns to look at me with blank eyes that only have the tiniest of dots of black in their center. "Only when dealing with something of this sensitive nature, Miss Corson." Her voice sounds almost alien to me. I don't know what her accent is, but English can't be her first language. Every word seems foreign to her except when she's reciting one of those funky spells of hers. "The authorities keep crime scenes restricted for a reason. We are only allowing Dr. Pythagoras to do this because I respect his intellect."

"This isn't a crime scene, though. Captain Tomorrow died miles from here."

"And yet Dr. Pythagoras chose to begin his investigation here."

Throughout our conversation, Rosey whistles to himself and taps on walls and floors. Every once in a while he bends over to investigate a seemingly empty nook or cranny, then straightens out and makes a humming noise as though whatever he just noticed is the most interesting thing in the world. I don't know what he's seeing, but it's nice to see him active. He's not only stretching his muscles, but his mind as well.

Captain Tomorrow's home—or, more accurately, Kingston Claremont's home—is a decent-sized house, but nothing all that gaudy. Apparently, in his double life, the Captain was a tenured history professor at Masters University. Usually, that would be a bad career for a vigilante to have, since there are so many deadlines and tight schedules to navigate. But for a time traveler, I suppose it would be easy to make a hectic teaching schedule your bitch.

Still, looking at the place brings up one thing that's always confused me about these people: they have the potential for all the wealth and prestige in the world, and yet they seem content to live firmly in the middle class, holding down a civilian job and all. While the house does have some nice features, like a bay window in the living room and hardwood floors, it's nothing to write home about. Captain Tomorrow had the ability to travel anywhere in time, but he chose to spend his life as a history professor in the suburbs, not even owning the nicest place on the block. Why not recover a couple Egyptian artifacts and live like a king for decades instead of letting yourself wallow in mediocrity?

Of course, he must have come into some money from somewhere, because he does have a few odds and ends here that let us know he really was a superhero. Several false walls pivot to reveal secret closets. The police left them open, revealing spare costumes and fancy chromed gadgetry. Rosey sighs when he comes across the first of them, disappointed that he didn't have a chance to unravel the superhero's secrets for himself.

"Are you sure you found all of these?" he asks the detective.

"I, um..." The middle-aged woman looks startled that Rosey's speaking to her and begins to stammer.

"I knew Kingston very well," Miss Destiny interrupts. "And I scried the home, just in case."

"So unless he knows how to ward off your magic, there's nothing here for me to find," Rosey notes.

"Don't you mean, 'knew,' Dr. Pythagoras?" I ask. "'Knew,' not 'knows?'"

"Knows," he insists. "He's a time traveler, moving in a nonlinear quantum direction. Just because the rest of us go straight down the street without taking that left turn at Albuquerque doesn't mean he can't slip into and out of the alleys."

"So is he dead or not?"

"Oh, he's dead. But where was he before he died? Did he pop off to the 23rd century, or slip back to the Dark Ages?"

I turn to Miss Destiny. "Was he on any missions you knew about?"

She blinks at me, which seems like a shrug. "Paradigm spoke to him last, not I. And we have both given all our information to the authorities."

"If you're not going to help, then why are you even letting us investigate?" I snap.

"Don't worry about it, Eva." Rosey says, climbing onto a wooden table and investigating the light fixtures. "I don't like looking up the answers in the back of the book anyway."

Miss Destiny gives me a sideways glance and purses her lips slightly. I tilt my head trying to figure out what that's supposed to mean. The witch makes every tiny movement seem like it has major significance.

Meanwhile, Rosey's in another world entirely. If he thinks there's even a possibility that the super-powered magician he once punched through a wall has something up her sleeve, he doesn't show it. Instead, he plucks a six-inch cylinder out of one of Captain Tomorrow's hidden closets and shakes it. The cylinder extends to a body-length rod that buzzes with electrical energy. With another shake, the item returns to its original size. My eyes can't even follow the movement of the device...it's like the staff just appears from some other dimension, then disappears, replaced by the tiny cylinder.

"Interesting," Rosey muses. "I don't think he ever...I mean, I don't think I ever saw him wield this on television."

"We all have our secrets, do we not?" Miss Destiny says. She tries to fix Rosey with a look designed to unsettle him, but he's already gone back to poking through the dead man's possessions.

"The deal was to give him a chance to be useful," I murmur, leaning in close to Miss Destiny. "If you're going to try to unnerve him and jerk him around, you should have let me know right away. Then I wouldn't have bothered to waste his time—or mine."

"Your time?" she retorts with something approaching sarcasm in her voice. "Do you plan to break any other supervillains out of jail, Miss Corson?"

"Screw you." I step forward and raise my voice. "Dr. Pythagoras, let's get out of here. We're being given the run-around."

Rosey picks up one of Tomorrow's spare goggles and looks through the lenses before shaking his head. "Oh, I know."

"Then why are we here?"

"Because we're looking for something the police—or Captain Tomorrow's allies—wouldn't have thought of."

I glance at Miss Destiny. The corners of her ruby lips curl downward. "What do you mean by that, Doctor?"

Rosey totters off to the kitchen without answering. Miss Destiny walks delicately, making no sound as she moves after him. I don't bother with stealth, and neither do the police who follow us, their hands on their guns the whole time. When we step into the kitchen, we find Rosey with his head poked into an open oven.

"I know none of you trust me...except you, of course, Eva," he calls from inside the appliance. "You're trying to see if I can scratch up some leads while also giving me enough rope to hang myself with." He finally removes his head from the oven. "But the trick is you're all assuming I want to find out who killed Captain Tomorrow. The police will figure that out. Right, officers?" He continues without waiting for a response from the officers. "I just want to know how it was possible that Captain Tomorrow died in the first place."

"The autopsy report would tell you that, Doctor," Miss Destiny says. "He was stabbed repeatedly, from what I remember."

"No, that's not what I'm after." He opens the refrigerator and breathes sharply in, apparently trying to deduce what sort of leftovers Captain Tomorrow kept. "I want to know how somebody could kill Mr. Claremont here and why it happened now of all times. The man can predict the future. Heck, to him, the future was part of days past. One of the reasons I—or rather, my clone—never managed to kill him is because he knew everything his enemies were about to do before they do it. So why didn't he see this one coming?"

When none of us provides him with an answer, Rosey sighs and half-sits, half-crouches on the floor. "There's something very strange about this place."

"You mean aside from the million hidden panels in the walls?" I ask.

"Yeah. There's something I'm missing…something everyone's missed so far."

Still bouncing around like he has the attention of a goldfish, Rosey practically dashes out of the kitchen, leaving us to chase after him. He scampers back to the living room and closes the pivoting walls one by one, returning the place to a normal-looking home. An average visitor wouldn't see a superhero lair—just a nice house with lots of blank space.

"He didn't keep any decorations here," I say. "No family portraits, no paintings, nothing."

Miss Destiny's eyes twitch and she looks at me, aghast that I would have the nerve to serve a purpose here other than just watch Rosey at work. Rosey, on the other hand, gives me a look of admiration.

"Good observation, Eva. I might not have caught that without you." He rubs a hand across one of the plain walls. "In fact, there are no souvenirs here at all. We're dealing with a man who met Helen of Troy in person, who viewed alien civilizations, and who made stops everywhere in between. You'd think he would keep a little something to commemorate it all. Tell the truth, Miss Destiny, you keep trophies, don't you? Little mementos or totems from your clashes with hoary hordes of demons or whatever else you magic types deal with?"

Miss Destiny bites the inside of her lip and says nothing.

"There's nothing wrong with remembering your victories," Rosey continues. I feel my heart flutter out of fear that he's about to mention some hidden trophy room of his own, but he stops himself from going any further.

"Maybe the apartment's just a front," I suggest. "Maybe he had a secret lair somewhere else." I face Miss Destiny, who looks more uncomfortable by the moment. It must suck to be on supervillain watch duty while Paradigm and the other heroes of Masters City are off fighting real crime. "That's what you guys do, right? He should have a Tomorrow Cave somewhere behind a waterfall."

"He could have just kept this place as a front for his secret identity. On the other hand, why go through all the trouble of trying to seem like a normal human if you aren't going to have something to show off your personality? Who has the money for nice things like this but no keepsakes or souvenirs?"

Rosey stops in front of the bookshelf and starts scanning through the encyclopedias. Between a small reference section and the beginning of what looks to be a lot of Jules Verne novels, a single knick-knack draws his attention. It looks like a Faberge egg, made entirely of silver and sitting in a wooden holder.

"Then there's this," he says, picking the egg up. "The only ornament in the entire place. Do you have anything you'd like to share, Miss De—"

The egg interrupts the musings with a high-pitched whirring noise. Crackles of blue lightning circle around it, and then surround Rosey. I give a yell and lunge forward, trying to knock the object out of his hands. I'm too slow. In half a second, he's gone, leaving a puff of gray smoke and nothing else behind.

"Rosey?" I feel my body shaking, and I tell myself to stop it. Just because I don't know what's happened doesn't mean I should panic.

The police have their guns out now, but it's not like shooting air can do anything. Miss Destiny steps forward, taking charge with a loud, authoritative voice.

"Everybody stand back. I can find out what has happened." She holds her hands upwards, her fingers twitching as she starts to sign something in the air. "By the Crimson Seekers of—"

Another whirring noise interrupts Miss Destiny's spell, and an electric crackle follows it. I realize just in time that I'm standing on the same spot where Rosey disappeared, and I jump back as more blue lightning begins to flash.

Barely maintaining my balance as my high heels almost betray me, I look back and find Rosey standing in front of the bookshelf again, slack-jawed and pale-faced but otherwise none the worse for wear.

"Dr. Pythagoras? Are you okay?"

He turns to face me, hearing my voice but not understanding the words. He opens his mouth once, then twice, closing it both times without uttering anything. Then he shakes his head, dusting cobwebs away and returning to the man I know.

"I'm not entirely sure what happened." He smiles with those words.

"We should get you checked out immediately," says Miss Destiny, waving the police back and forming a window with her thumbs and forefingers as she starts a mystic examination of my client.

"No need," Rosey says, waving her away and stepping toward me. "I'm fine. And I'm done here." He marches past me and toward the door. "We're on the right track," he whispers to me on his way by.

The police stand about awkwardly, looking at Miss Destiny for instruction. She shrugs her shoulders and begins her own investigation, scanning everything in the apartment once more with her magic to see if she can figure out what else she might have missed. I grin and leave, walking with Rosey back to my car.

#5: FUTURE PAST

On my thirtieth birthday, I decided to block out the sun.

I had already clashed with Paradigm numerous times by then, always losing and only escaping by the skin of my teeth. The wealth I had accumulated with my patents and research kept me safe from the law, shielded in the high corporate towers of RP Industries, but Paradigm could leap those skyscrapers and find me wherever I hid. Moreover, he seemed to have targeted me specifically, going out of his way to kick sand in my face—another bully lining up to take shots at the smart kid.

It took me years to realize why he hated me, which is almost shameful considering how simple the answer was. Unlike everyone else he had encountered over the decades—Nazis and Soviets and giant monsters—I had the potential to beat him. I hadn't managed it yet, but one day my keen wit would pierce his invulnerable hide. One day, a mortal man would be able to take him down. That terrified him, and his terror became hatred.

When aliens from the twelfth dimension invaded Masters City, they challenged Paradigm enough to make him bleed. Sure, it was only a light scratch on his cheek, but it was probably more pain than he had felt in decades. From the small sample of his blood I collected, I learned a few key facts that even my research hadn't yet uncovered. Most importantly, the sun made Paradigm more powerful.

That's not to say he was a solar-powered superhero or anything of the sort. His own body had the power of an exploding atomic bomb regardless. But the sun augmented his already formidable strength and endurance, making his skin diamond hard and giving him the strength needed to toss a baseball to Jupiter.

So the plan was simple: take away the sun, and I could bring him down to Earth a little bit. It wouldn't kill him, but it would shave some of his advantage away—close the gap between brain and brawn enough for me to finally secure a victory over him.

If the sun's the problem, take it out of the equation. When a door closes, don't go through the open window. Turn the closed door into an interdimensional portal instead. Being a supervillain is about vision, not logic. In a world of time travel, nuclear men, and mutants, you can bend the rules to make them fit what you want.

But even when tweaking the laws of physics, outright destroying the sun is a terrible idea. I might have been unbalanced, but I had no desire to bring about the apocalypse. Pulling the Earth's moon out of orbit and causing a solar eclipse using a proton beam powered by the energy of the planet's core, though...that was fair game. A few tidal waves here and there, some gravitational abnormalities...I calculated everything to minimize the loss of life around the globe. But the crime was also big enough to get the attention of Paradigm, to lure him to my lair when he was at his weakest.

Naturally, Paradigm wouldn't come out to play on his own. Knowing I'd have a trap set for him, he sent one of his allies first...Captain Tomorrow. The same Captain Tomorrow who fell into my quantum force field almost immediately and became my prisoner. Also the same Captain Tomorrow whose house I was in not more than two seconds ago, before I accidentally picked up a time travel device left just for me.

The Faberge egg disappears in a burst of white smoke as I rematerialize in the chamber where I held Captain Tomorrow prisoner. My lair at this point lay several miles below the Earth's crust, drawing power from the magma of the planet's core. The cold, sterile room lacked a human touch that I still haven't really grown to care for. Metal floors and ceilings, some nice swivel chairs, and a computer system the size of a double-wide trailer...that's the way I like it.

On one screen, graphics displaying the moon's trajectory informs me of the experiment's progress. I never saw these readings—at the moment, based on the explosions and tremors elsewhere in the compound, the past-me is commanding battle droids to deal with Paradigm and the League of Liberty who have come together to protect him.

"Roosevelt," Captain Tomorrow says from the seven-by-seven square that serves as his cell. It almost looks like he could just leave, except for the occasional flashes of white static where my carefully calibrated quantum field hems him in. "I know why you're here."

"Interesting." I glance at my now-empty hand before closing to within a few paces of the cell. I make sure to stay out of arm's reach. Just because he shouldn't be able to penetrate the quantum field doesn't mean he can't. "I don't remember meeting another me here, and you'll remain trapped until Miss Destiny finds the ancient Egyptian ankh that's been dampening her powers."

"You have a good memory."

"Considering the head trauma I've suffered over the years, I'll consider that an accomplishment. And..." I pause, then laugh. "Of course. My memory's even better than I thought it was."

I walk over to the main console, where a mug of peppermint cappuccino and a half-eaten donut sits next to a dog-eared lab book. Flipping the cover open, I retrieve a fountain pen and write a message on the first page.

A clone did it.

Four simple words that wouldn't become clear until years later when I had finally been captured and needed to grab desperately onto something to serve as a feeble defense. I had always assumed I wrote it down in a fit of insomnia.

I put the pen down and close the lab book. Turning back toward Captain Tomorrow, I shake my head in disappointment. He's not the least bit surprised to see that he inadvertently gave me the means to break out of prison. That means I'm playing right into his plans.

"So?" I snap. "Why have you brought me here? Am I to play a role in my own defeat?"

"Your petty plans are doomed to failure," he says like he's reading from a script. "They always are."

"Petty?" I gesture toward the screen. Side monitors have lit up now, showing how the moon's motion alters the tides, causing typhoons and whirlpools throughout the Pacific Ocean. "I'm pulling the moon out of orbit and blocking out the sun for a period of hours. And in case you've gone deaf in there, I'm holding my own against an assembly of superpowered freaks, all using nothing but my own brain! Call my plans what you want, but don't call them petty."

"We don't have time for this. There's a reason I set that object out for you."

"As far as I'm concerned, that reason is all a part of my new job. I have an opportunity most police and investigators never get: I get to ask the dead man what killed him."

He hesitates, and what little I can see of his face grows pale. "What...what are you talking about?"

There it is—the flicker of doubt that a man who knows the future should never have. His voice wavers, his hands tremble. He gets it under control quickly, but in that split-second I find two things I've never seen in him before: a moment of surprise, and a fear of the unknown. I squint, examining the lines of his face and body language to figure out what he's trying to hide from me.

Unfortunately, all I see is the part of his chin not covered by his cowl and goggles. That's because of a rule I swore never to break: never unmask a hero. It wastes valuable time when you've got them captured, and it makes you a threat to be dealt with immediately. Stay on neutral ground, and they'll most likely let you escape and fight another day. Get in a position to ruin their personal lives and hurt their loved ones, though, and they'll hunt you to the ends of the Earth.

I watch him Captain Tomorrow. He watches me back, searching for some clue as to what I mean. When he finds that I won't give him any more information, he goes back to his usual banter.

"The person you see here isn't the person I was yesterday or even the day before," he says. "I move constantly through the time stream, jumping to wherever I'm needed."

"Right. Your tomorrow is my yesterday, but next week for you might be twenty years into my future. But you left that device in your home for me. You knew I'd be there. Did you know why?"

He licks his lips and says nothing. I laugh—only a short outburst for right now. I'll save the good stuff for later.

"You're a dead man, Captain! In all your trips to the future, didn't you ever think to look at a newspaper once in a while?"

"Someone has meddled with my temporal senses," he says gravely. "The implications of that alone should convince you to drop this case."

"I can't drop the case, my dear Captain. Solving this mystery is part of my terms of release."

"Talk to that lawyer friend of yours, Pythagoras. She got you out of prison; she can get you off the case. Other mysteries will come along, but this one has no solution for you or anybody else. If you stay on this path, you'll be headed somewhere much worse than a cell. And you'll bring hundreds of people along with you."

An explosion rattles the base. My kamikaze-bot just laid a heck of a blow on Paradigm. I can hear Miss Destiny screaming his name, mixing in with the sound of my laughter.

"Stay aware, kiddo," I mutter to past-me. "She's about to break one of her sacred vows and momentarily banish you to the fifth circle of Hell."

"Roosevelt, are you listening to me?" my prisoner asks.

"I always wondered why I liked you," I reply to him. "I mean, look at you right now. I could have put mind-controlling nanites into you and turned you against your allies. Instead I just kept you in a cage for a while. And now that I see you here, now that you've yanked me out of my own time, I can see why. You always treated this eternal struggle like business instead of treating it personally like Paradigm did. And now I'm guessing the reason you always did that is because you knew how it was all going to end…or, at least, you thought you did."

"Roosevelt…right now, you're at a crucial stage in your life. You can do anything from here. You can finally put that brain of yours to good use, or you can make the same mistakes you've always made."

From behind the reinforced doors, a familiar shout in my voice: "Curses! You stupid meddling heroes!"

"Listen to that," Captain Tomorrow continues. "You can keep doing this forever, or you can set yourself on a new course. Walk away now, while you can, and be a hero for a change."

"You keep talking to me like you know the future, but you're missing key facts."

"What facts?"

"One," I start counting my points on my fingers, "I had a revelation in prison. I realized how much time I've wasted fighting superheroes instead of using my brain and money to cure cancer or put a man on Mars. I get that one of the primary reasons I wanted to kill Paradigm was because his death was a puzzle to be solved. If you know anything about me now as opposed to me in the past, you know I've moved on to other puzzles.

"Two, you haven't told me anything about the clone-me or the time-displaced-me or whatever it is. Either you're in the dark just like I am or you know something you won't tell me. That makes it hard for me to take your advice seriously.

"And three, you don't know the most important fact of all—the fact that you died this week, and it played a key role in my release. So the future you see is different from the present I know. And honestly, what's more useless than a time traveler who can't even keep his alternate futures straight?"

"It's not an alternate future, Roosevelt. You need to listen to what I'm saying. I'm trying to warn you—"

"No offense Captain, but your warnings are a waste of my time." I turn as a super-strong fist starts pounding at the door, buckling it inwards. It's not Paradigm—he's been weakened too much by this point. But he brought along the Blue Bull, one of his buddies from the League of Liberty. "Now, since I don't recall meeting myself during the battle, I assume our time together is just about done." On cue, the blue lightning that brought me here starts surrounding my body again. "I need to get back to figuring out how you died."

He shouts something at me as I vanish entirely. With a nauseating feeling that resembles airsickness, I find myself back where I stood before, with a very surprised Eva standing next to me.

"Dr. Pythagoras? Are you okay?"

I turn to answer her, but find myself lacking words.

I open my mouth to tell her about the lecture I got from Captain Tomorrow, but close it again. I'll have to think over what he said and give it some analysis.

I open my mouth again to tell her about the more important discovery: that the seemingly omniscient time traveler doesn't even have his own timeline straight. But again I stay silent. If that's the case, what does it mean? Who has the power to interfere with Captain Tomorrow's abilities?

Finally, I shake my head and focus on the one fact I actually know. "I'm not entirely sure what happened."

I smile with those words. It's going to be fun finding out.

#6: SECRET IDENTITIES

Some people jump off rooftops to get a hero's attention. I just wait for them to come to me.

My penthouse apartment sports comfortable leather furniture, stylish objets d'art, and a balcony that offers a great view of the cityscape. The one thing it lacks is any trace of supers. All my trophies and pictures are at the office. At home, I don't want any reminders that the flights and tights even exist. Unfortunately, even in my off hours, I'm still working.

I'm on the balcony sipping my second glass of chardonnay when I hear movement inside. I hope she came through the door, but I didn't hear the knob turn. I finish my glass before moving to meet her.

"Did he tell you anything?" Miss Destiny asks.

"He's asked to view Captain Tomorrow's corpse."

"That can be arranged," she says. "Is there anything else?"

"You know the deal. I'm not talking to you. Let her out."

"I am the one best equipped to deal with Dr. Pythagoras."

"No," I say. "That would be me. And you're either going to play by my rules or we won't play."

"Very well," she sighs. Closing her eyes, she traces a six-pointed star in the air and mutters the magic word, "Mhasaz."

A burst of purple mist sets off my smoke alarms, but thankfully not the sprinklers. It smells vaguely of peppermint.

"Sorry," comes a teenage voice from behind the haze. "She wouldn't make the change outside."

When the smoke clears and the alarm stops screeching, Miss Destiny has vanished. In her place is a plump 16-year-old girl dressed in a t-shirt, sweatpants, and sandals. I smile and put my hand on her shoulder.

"Would you like a cup of cocoa, Mei?"

As near as either of us can figure out, Mei became bonded with the Destiny Entity nine years ago, becoming the youngest host in history. Not that Miss Destiny's past is all that well-recorded, of course. She claims to have existed since at least the Middle Ages, but nobody can corroborate her story.

"So he wants to see Captain Tomorrow." She wipes away a foam mustache from the cocoa. "Seems kind of weird to me. If I got to choose one corpse to see, I'd probably choose my own. Figure out how I'm gonna die, y'know?"

"Technically we don't know it's Rosey's corpse there. It could be a clone."

"I thought you said you made the clone story up."

I give Mei a look that could curdle milk. She hunches her shoulders and sinks down in her chair.

"Sorry," she whispers.

I raise my cup to my lips and take a slow sip. After a moment of silence between us, I pick up the conversation again. "I said the clone story might be more complicated than what I've presented in court. We don't know for sure what this other Roosevelt is. That's the problem with this world—you've always got to account for the impossible."

"Anyway," Mei says, "no matter what it is, I'd totally want to take a look at my own body. Maybe I could pick up something important to keep myself safe."

I push my mug aside and take a moment to enjoy the smell of chocolate. It's not as relaxing as I'd like it to be. "If time travel is involved, you'd want to stop yourself from dying."

"Yeah," she replies. "I mean, who wouldn't?"

"Hopefully, Rosey has his eye on the bigger picture," I respond. "It's not about him. It's about showing what he can do for society—what anybody in his position can do if they get a second chance."

Mei furrows her brow. "You don't want him to save himself?"

I glare at my mug, walk to the kitchenette, and dump the rest of my drink down the sink.

"Okay," Mei calls after me, "then what do you want him to do?"

I consider pouring myself another chardonnay, but instead come back into the dining room empty-handed. Mei still hasn't gone back to her own cocoa.

"I want the same thing you want: a situation where everybody wins."

Mei raises her eyebrows. "Everybody? Even Paradigm?"

"He can win too if he shuts up and doesn't think with his ego," I reply. Then I start ticking off potential wins on my fingers. "Rosey proves he's the hero he always envisioned himself as. I prove that anybody can be reformed. The police find Captain Tomorrow's killer. And you finally get to go free."

Mei smiles—or starts to. The smile flickers out, leaving her face gloomier than before, like a bulb has burned out in her mind. She puts her hands flat on the table and rests her chin on top of them.

"Yeah...but what if maybe that's not what should happen?"

"Which part?"

"You know which part."

With a scrape across the hardwood floor, I push my chair closer to Mei's and put my hand on her cheek. "I know what you think you deserve. But remember—you're making amends. That's why you bonded with Miss Destiny. And what better source is there to know when you've made up for your past than the mystical spirit of justice itself?"

Mei doesn't move. She doesn't acknowledge my touch. She just stares ahead, eyes black and dead.

"I don't think I want to talk about this anymore."

"Okay. Why don't we—"

"Sorry."

"That's okay. We just—"

"Mhasaz."

The burst of smoke clears away faster this time. When the haze clears, Miss Destiny still sits in Mei's position. I still have my hand resting gently on the side of her face. We both correct ourselves quickly, standing up and taking a few paces away from each other.

"Mei will be alright," Miss Destiny says in that unrecognizable accent of hers. "She is closer than she thinks."

"She needs a psychiatrist, not a superhero."

"We all have many things we need, Miss Corson. But our only choice is to deal with the things we have. Mei has me. Dr. Pythagoras has you. And we should focus on helping him if we want to help her."

"Like I said, he wants to see Captain Tomorrow's body."

"And as I said, that can be arranged. Did he tell you why?"

I shrug. "Dr. Pythagoras never tells anybody why he does things. Just don't go telling me he's not going to find anything your people couldn't. If that's the case, you're just wasting everybody's time by letting him take part in the investigation."

"Believe me, Miss Corson. I want him to succeed as badly as you do. Then Mei can get what she deserves. And perhaps Dr. Pythagoras can, too."

"Whatever," I say sourly. "Let's just deal with business. You'll get permission for him to continue the investigation?"

"I see no harm in doing so." Her eyes narrow. "Although I do find the way you are asking to be quite peculiar."

I start to feel an itch on my back, right in that annoying place under my bra strap that I can never reach. "That's all well and good. I don't care."

"You are asking me to get permission," she observes. "Not telling me. And you asked for a private meeting with Mei rather than dealing with this matter by telephone."

"You can leave now."

"Mei did not tell you what you wanted to hear, did she?"

"The only thing I want to hear from Mei is that she's over her parents' death. And to tell you the truth, I don't think that's ever going to happen."

"And now you are evading my question. Something is odd here indeed."

I point to the door. "Get out. Do your damned job and I'll do mine."

She starts walking, and I foolishly allow myself the hope that she'll follow my instructions. But she stops before opening the door and turns around. Her mouth seems crooked, although I can't tell if she's smiling or frowning.

"You asked Mei here to talk things out with her," she says. "You want to comply with Dr. Pythagoras' request, and yet at the same time you do not. What is it you are afraid of him discovering? Or are you just afraid of him? Do you think letting him this deep into our mystery will bring out the worst in him?"

"I'm not afraid of Rosey," I snap. "At least not in the same way you're afraid of Paradigm."

She bows her head, allowing me my victory. "Very well. I will leave you to your worries if you leave me to mine. We will speak again tomorrow."

With that, she says a magic word, waves her hands, and disappears in a flash of light.

Damned supers. The door was right there, and she just couldn't walk through it, could she?

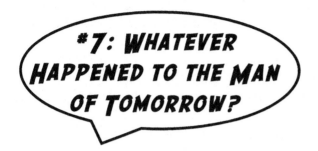

#7: WHATEVER HAPPENED TO THE MAN OF TOMORROW?

*O*nce you start down the long and wonderful world of mad science, nobody ever fully trusts you again.

Apparently, "access to the body" means I get to stand in the same room as the corpse and glance at it. Policemen in body armor lurk within arm's reach at all times. A medical examiner takes over for my sense of touch, exposing wounds when I ask her to but making it quite clear that I cannot make physical contact with the body. Miss Destiny stands nearby, arms folded and looking terse.

"I told you, I wound up flashing back some years into the past," I explain, figuring half a truth might win her over a little. "Captain Tomorrow tried to warn me about something, but he was obviously as confused as I was."

She blinks her eyes three times and my body lights up with a bluish glow. She probably calls it reading my aura. I call it watching my bioelectrical field for drastic changes. Regardless of the terminology, though, it's her mystical lie detector, and everybody in the room can see it.

"If you are hiding something, Dr. Pythagoras, I will know," Miss Destiny says.

"I realize that. Captain Tomorrow had obviously keyed the object to my DNA, which gave me the opportunity to speak with our victim here. But the whole experience was useless, since he didn't know he was dead in our time. He mentioned that somebody had blocked his temporal senses. My personal theory is—"

With another blink of her eyes and a wave of her hand, the aura around me fades away. "I do not need to hear theories right now, Doctor. We shall speak more about the incident in the future, I am sure."

"So I can get to work?"

"Under the restrictions you agreed to, yes."

"It's the best we could do, Rosey," Eva remarks. "You're lucky we're here at all."

"Who's complaining? I'm not complaining." I kneel down and start rummaging through my backpack.

Back in high school, I sometimes cut class so I could sneak over to the elementary playground and spend time with people my own age. My father always thought my big brain was his ticket out of poverty. If he knew about slacking in my studies, he would have given me a black eye.

I wonder how he's doing in that alien zoo where I left him.

Since I didn't belong among them, I rarely got to play with those kids. Only once did I ever get invited into a game of pretend. We had to play superheroes, of course. Cops and Robbers doesn't have the same appeal as pretending to be vigilantes in tights. The biggest of the boys got to play Paradigm, and my scrawny self got left playing the evil robot known as the Iron Brain.

"Surrender, fiend!" With the other villains defeated, the Paradigm-boy jumped from atop the monkey bars and nearly kept his balance, only slightly embarrassed as he toppled onto his bottom.

"Um...no," I replied as the dark-haired goliath picked himself up to tower over me.

"You have to surrender," he admonished. "I'm made of atomic power."

"Ah, but I have...um...the entropy ray!"

The ogre's eyes bulged out and he clenched his fists at my defiance. "That's stupid. There's no such thing."

"How do you know?" I asked. "The Iron Brain has an IQ of two thousand or something and lives in an alien ship on Venus."

"But he's never used an entropy ray."

"Not that you know about. But have you ever been to Venus?"

"You don't even know what that ray thingy does!"

"Yeah I do. It...um...it speeds up the process of entropy, of course."

"That's stupid," the boy growled, irritated with my obstinance. "You're just making words up."

"No I'm not." My voice began to mimic the professional yet condescending tone of my professors. "No thermodynamic process can keep producing energy infinitely. If you could speed up the process by which disorder gets introduced into the system, you could make it all fall apart. Even superpowers have their limits."

"Nuh-uh. Paradigm's older than my grandpa, and he's still super."

"But he's still powered by energy, and he's still subject to the second law of thermodynamics. No energy reaction works perfect. Now, if we hypothesize the source of Paradigm's power as a closed system, then the entropy ray can—"

My theorizing came to an abrupt end as the boy's fist collided with my face.

My vision went black. I came to on my back, with tears in my eyes and blood on my face.

"Beat that, brainiac," the boy said as he and his friends walked away.

If anyone said anything else, I didn't hear them. I only heard the other children laughing at me.

I've spent my entire life fighting different kinds of bullies. Some kids get freakishly large at the age of eight, others shoot lasers from their fingertips. They could hurt me, but they couldn't stop me from playing my games. My inventions moved from playground theory to scientific fact, giving me the power to match forces against living gods. Even the entropy ray is still somewhere in the attic of my brain, waiting for me to blow dust off of it and give it new life.

My main tool for this part of the investigation is a simple pair of glasses. The lenses look brownish-yellow to everyone else in the room, but they allow me to see clear as day.

"Sunglasses?" Eva asks.

"No," I answer. "Once upon a time, there was a superhero named Eagle Eye. Born with uncanny vision, he became an expert marksman and served in the Viet Nam War. He was big in his day—the American Paradigm had become an independent operator and dropped the 'American' part of his name following the McCarthy Era, and a lot of people started to fear the supposed heroes protecting them." I pause to think. People look upon that era as a dark chapter of history, but it doesn't sound so bad to me. "Folks liked Eagle Eye. He didn't run around in a colorful suit and tell kids to say no to drugs, and he didn't question the direction our country was going in. He just saw a bad guy and shot him."

"And what happened to him?"

"Nobody knows for sure. Maybe he got killed in action. Maybe he just got old. That's the thing about people who wear masks—you can just take them off one day and be somebody else. But I read about Eagle Eye, and I always liked the idea of being able to see like he did. So I built something to let me do it."

I tap on the corner of the frames and my vision snaps to a microscopic level. I can see every skin cell of Captain Tomorrow's corpse—every stray particle or subatomic hint that the killer might have left on his body.

I touch another part of the frames and things go back to normal. Look at his face first, I remind myself. This is a man whom I fought against for what seems like forever. Give him a little dignity.

His eyes closed and his face expressionless, Captain Tomorrow looks nothing like the man I spoke to just yesterday…or several years ago, whichever it was.

I only recognize the chin. His cowl concealed everything else. Even his eyes remained always hidden behind those mirrored goggles of his. His face is wrinkled and his hair has gone gray at the temples. His mouth is still in a perpetual frown, grim and determined even in death. I reach out to touch the man, but one of the guards clears his throat and clicks the safety off his gun.

"Of course," I mutter, getting back to work.

I tap the back of the metal frames twice, switching my vision to scan for different kinds of radiation. A variety of energy signatures show up in the room, each color-coded for my convenience. Captain Tomorrow's body is free of most of the ambient radiation, except for a silver sparkle on his skin. Glancing elsewhere in the room, everything seems normal, save for Miss Destiny. She's invisible to my goggles, hiding in her shroud of mysticism. Her magic and my technolgy never did mix very well. It's always been a blind spot for me.

"Could you point out the injuries, please?"

At my direction, the examiner exposes a series of bruises running from Tomorrow's neck down to his front torso. Looks like he got into a dust-up shortly before he died. Then the examiner rolls the body partway over to show me a set of four deep stab wounds on his back, each showing up as bright silver in my enhanced vision. Things apparently got more serious.

"I see. The entry wounds are narrow, but the blades managed to perforate his major organs." I take the goggles off and turn to Eva. "Who uses blades and is still active these days?"

Eva furrows her brow and goes through her mental rolodex. "Razorclaw's on probation."

"He's too sloppy. If he managed to get this close, he would have torn Tomorrow in half."

"The Green Knight hasn't been seen since a fight with Desperado about a year ago, but he hasn't been captured, either."

"Hm...a guy with a magical sword. Miss Destiny, are there any traces of magic on the body? I figure you're the sorceress supreme and all, so you'd know best."

She softens a little bit at the flattery, mostly because of the charming clumsiness with which I applied it. Whispering a magical incantation to herself, she stares at Captain Tomorrow's corpse.

Miss Destiny starts to speak, then pauses as though something caught her tongue. She clears her throat and tries again. "No…nor was there any when I checked last."

"And when was that?" I ask.

"When he and you—or rather, your 'clone'—turned up dead in the first place."

"Darn," I mutter. "Green Knight would have been a convenient guy to blame. But it doesn't quite fit with the other evidence anyway."

"What about someone who can stab from a range?" Eva asks, still brainstorming. "The Silk Stiletto is at large, and she's a pretty good shot with her knives."

"I'm afraid a thrown weapon isn't likely because of the bruising pattern around the wounds. That's what you found, right?"

I glance up at the medical examiner long enough to see her nod, then turn my attention back to the body.

"And it all happened so fast he couldn't stop it. That means somebody with super speed. Even with a nice long, sharp piece of metal like the killer used, Captain Tomorrow wouldn't have died instantly. Have you ever cut into a jack-o'-lantern, Eva?"

"Yeah. Why?"

"If you just stab into it with a blade, you can't easily yank it back out. It gets stuck. A person's skin isn't as thick as a pumpkin's, but the body is dense enough that you can't stick a knife in that deeply, then pull it out and do it again, all while a combat-trained victim doesn't even turn around or try to run away."

"Maybe there's a new super in town we don't know about," Eva offers.

"Perhaps." I nod, but remain unconvinced.

"So are we back to square one?" Eva asks.

"Not at all." I take off the goggles. "Is it possible to see one more corpse?"

"You're only authorized for this one, sir," the medical examiner says. "This is part of an ongoing investigation. I can't really give just anybody access to these things. And besides—"

Miss Destiny cuts her off with a wave of her hand. "I might be able to clear it, so long as Dr. Pythagoras continues his willingness to abide by our restrictions—and gives me a thorough account of his time travel yesterday."

"My client's not about to discuss anything of that sort," Eva responds.

"It's okay, Eva. I don't have any useful information for Miss Destiny, so she can pick my brain all she wants—with you in the room, of course, and after I view the second corpse."

Miss Destiny looks through me, staring in my general direction but with eyes that seem like they're watching something a thousand miles away. Then she nods and refocuses.

"And whose body did you wish to examine, Dr. Pythagoras?" Miss Destiny asks.

"Mine, of course."

"Yours?"

"My clone's, to be specific."

Eva's eyes narrow. "Let's step outside for a second and talk in private."

I return the goggles to my backpack. "Of course."

Once we're out of earshot of the supervisory crew, Eva fixes me with one of her stern looks that tells me I'll have to explain what I'm thinking before she lets me play any longer. "You never mentioned wanting to get a look at the clone's corpse," she says lowly. "Why now?"

"There's less evidence than I hoped," I answer. "So now I'd like to know how the other me died. Assuming the two deaths are linked, looking at the second corpse might fill us in as to what happened to the first one."

She touches my shoulder and bends forward, leaning close enough to whisper into my ear. "You have a habit of thinking out loud when you get working. You mention anything that gets the guards thinking the body isn't really a clone of you, and you'll wind up right back in jail."

"Don't worry about it," I reply. "I can keep my mouth shut about important facts."

She shoots me a skeptical look. "You can?"

"Absolutely. I didn't mention the biggest clue I found on Captain Tomorrow's corpse, did I?"

"What clue is that?"

"The wounds had traces of gamma radiation around them."

"And what's so significant about that?"

"Gamma is the type of radiation you see in atomic decay," I say, unconsciously slipping into my professor voice. "It's common enough, but not in the concentration near those wounds. And there are only a few things on this planet that could leave that specific level of energy signature. Combine that with the fact that the killer was smart enough to know exactly where to hit, as well as strong and fast enough to drive the blades up to their hilt and then strike again almost instantly, and there's only a few conclusions I can draw."

Eva's face turns a little ashen as she starts following my thought process. "I thought you said there wasn't enough evidence."

"I said there was less evidence than I hoped. Not enough to draw a firm conclusion, but enough to form a hypothesis."

"So what's your hypothesis?" she asks. "Who's your prime suspect?"

I fidget a little, adjusting the strap on my sack-o'-technology. "I think it's me."

#8: FUTURE IMPERFECT

*H*ow can you trust a supervillain to keep his mouth shut? I almost turn blue holding my breath, expecting Rosey to blow the whole scheme with his incessant need to let other people know how clever he is.

I wait, and wait, and wait. The room hums with the buzz of air conditioning and the slow, measured breaths of Miss Destiny, who looks like she's entering some sort of meditative trance. Rosey doesn't bother speaking to the medical examiner; he just gestures vaguely when he wants the body moved.

I ponder the proper defense while waiting for the dam of silence to burst. We were in Captain Tomorrow's home, he touched that silver egg-thing, he disappeared for a few minutes and came back obviously shaken. Bam—he's potentially post-trauma right now. Unfortunately, he's been acting perfectly fine until this point, so spinning his inevitable mad tirade will be difficult.

Rosey bends over his own face, examining the corpse's open eyes. He's so close that I almost think he's going to kiss the dead man. But then he pulls back, glances in my direction, and smiles before returning to his examination.

I check my watch. I've got a meeting with another client this afternoon. I wonder how long it's going to take me to wheel and deal Rosey away from whatever jail cell he's about to land himself in.

Rosey stands up straight, folds his x-ray specs up, and tucks them back into his backpack. Then he looks at Miss Destiny with a lop-sided grin and says, "Cool."

"Cool?" she asks, raising an eyebrow as they start putting the dead doppelganger in a body bag. "I take it you discovered something?"

Here it comes. "I think I'd like to talk to him before he discloses anything," I start, positioning myself in between Rosey and Miss Destiny.

"It's fine, Eva. And no, I didn't really find much except what I'm sure you've all figured out right now: the clone died at the hands of the same person who did in Captain Tomorrow, with the same sharp implement. This one was a single stab through the heart. My clone, it seems, was the secondary target. That lines up with all your assumptions, correct?"

"Indeed it does. What, then is 'cool' about it?"

"Well, how often do you get to meet yourself face to face, even if the other you happens to be dead?"

"Approximately twice a week," Miss Destiny responds.

"Okay, you've got your funky witchcraft thing going on," Rosey says. "But it's new to me."

"And now you will tell me about your time travel experience?" she asks.

"Of course I will." Rosey touches me on the arm. "As long as my lawyer is present."

Seeing an aura-reading sorceress cross-examine my client actually worries me less than watching Rosey examine his "clone." Spells and other inexplicable magic mumbo-jumbo don't hold much water with a jury. Also, I have Mei on my side—an ally that not even Rosey knows about yet.

"What else did he say?" she asks, studying the aura around Rosey.

"His exact words: 'I'm trying to warn you...' Unfortunately, he got cut off before he got a chance to finish his sentence, and I wound up back in the future...er, present."

I scribble down a few notes on a legal pad, in case any of this gets used against him later. Then, with a sigh, Miss Destiny snaps her fingers and the aura disappears.

"You are telling the truth...or at least what you see as the truth. Captain Tomorrow wanted to warn you of something. It is a shame we do not know what he meant."

"Wasting words is a good way to get a brilliant plan to unravel in front of you...or so I've heard," Rosey says.

She nods, then walks away, not even bothering to say goodbye.

"Hey, Rosey..." I begin.

He perks up and smiles at me. "Yeah?"

"You did well in there," I tell him.

The corners of his lips turn upward. "I did?"

"You kept your mouth shut. I didn't really expect that out of you."

He stands on tiptoes, getting a little bit closer to my face. Then he rocks back to his heels again. "You told me not to say anything, Eva, so I didn't. Is that so hard to believe?"

"Coming from you? Yes."

"I'm not always a talker, you know," he says with an offended sniff. "Compared to most of my peers, I managed to keep my monologues pretty short. And I never once told a captured hero about the death trap I had just placed him in."

He blinks and walks part me, slinging his backpack over his shoulder and heading for the door with slumped shoulders. I narrow my eyes. Is he sulking?

I chase after him, catching him just outside. He keeps marching toward the curb, waving a hand to hail a taxi.

"Rosey, I didn't mean that as an insult to your intelligence."

"Hey, no problem," he mumbles.

"Don't catch a cab," I say. "I'll give you a ride."

"You will?"

"I'm your partner," I say, taking his arm and leading him toward my car. "I need to know what you found out, don't I?"

He pivots with me toward the underground parking garage where I left my car. "Fair enough."

"Good," I say. "So what did you find out?"

"I'm a dead man." He says it so cheerfully that it almost seems like he's mocking me.

"What?"

"That person is my genetic equal—not only the same DNA like a clone would have, but the same minor scars, even the same moles and receding hairline. Those things don't automatically happen with a clone. Well, the hairline might, but only at a certain point in life. The scars are too similar to be coincidental, and the moles represent an irregular growth of cells that shouldn't be duplicated in the exact same way."

I get walking again, practically dragging Rosey to my car. He might be good at staying quiet around the authorities, but he runs off at the mouth around me. It seems like he's always trying to impress me, and I don't need somebody overhearing that. Once we're in the car, I turn on some music to help make sure that even someone with super-hearing can't eavesdrop.

"So, like we both knew, the whole clone thing is bunk," I say.

"That's right," he confirms.

"Then what's your explanation for being in two places at once?"

"Time travel, of course."

I grip the wheel until my knuckles go white. "You keep mentioning time travel like a common thing, like it's just another form of public transportation."

"Oh, right," he says apologetically. "Sorry about that. Seeing as I just did a little time-hopping yesterday, I guess I'm kind of acquainted with it now. Let me explain a bit. Both the other-me and Captain Tomorrow had the same type of quantum radiation on the body—the energy used when Captain Tomorrow activates his powers. It seems very possible that I will be involved in some way with the death of Captain Tomorrow. At the very least, I'll be in proximity to him when it happens. There's no other way I know of that I would be pulled back to the same time as him during our respective deaths; his technology has always been keyed to his own genetic signature. Unless he's taking on students somewhere or somewhen, there's no way anybody else would be able to use his tools.

"As to the identity of the killer," he continues, "that might be me, but there's a problematic item in the lack of weaponry on my corpse. I would need something to enhance my strength and speed. Maybe my old battle suit, but that's bulky enough that it would have been noticed. Maybe if I—"

"Let's focus on one thing at a time," I interrupt before he starts running numbers in his head. "What does this mean for you?"

"Well, it means that somewhere in the near future, I'm a potential murderer. Is there a legal precedent for evil future versions of yourself committing murder in the present day?"

"Actually, yes," I groan. "*Pennsylvania v. The Centurion.* Basically, you can't be convicted of a crime you didn't commit yet. But it's a little sticky, because then the police know you will commit the crime, because if the court case changed the path you were on, the dead person wouldn't be dead because you never would have traveled back and killed him, and...oy."

"I know, I know." Rosey pats my shoulder sympathetically. "I find that generic-brand acetylsalicylic acid is the best way to deal with logic-based headaches. And anyway, it's not a slam-dunk that other-me committed the crime. Although now I do need to find myself access to a lab so I can figure out how to change the future, and I need to do it as soon as possible."

"Why as soon as possible?"

"Based on cell composition and degeneration, the other-me was about the same age as the real-me, give or take a few months. This means if I'm going to get killed and then thrown back into time, it's probably going to be sooner rather than later. I have no intention of letting that happen."

"Remember that you're investigating Captain Tomorrow's death. You need to save him, too."

"Of course, of course." He gives a dismissive wave of his hand. "Save the buffoon who couldn't fix the world with years of access to time travel, but ignore the plight of somebody who could actually do something great with the technology. The law is so insulting sometimes."

I smolder at Rosey, trying to keep him on task.

"Relax," he says. "If I save one, I probably save the other, too. And if I am the killer, I just have to keep my finger off the trigger—or the blade."

"Good." After a moment of thought, I add, "But if the future-you already traveled back into the past and died, then you can't really change the future, can you? Oh, my headache is getting worse."

"Time travel is confusing. I have nine PhDs, including one in quantum mechanics, and I still don't really get it. Theoretically, things in the future aren't really written yet—they're only potential futures until they happen. Probability-wise, the odds are I'm going to wind up dead in a short while. But if we can figure things out quickly enough to stop it, that probability becomes an alternate future—a separate timeline from our reality, where we manage to stop this from happening."

"But if you stop it from happening because you knew it was going to happen—"

"Then we get into paradox territory," Rosey explains, far too calmly for my liking.

"And has that happened before?"

"Theoretically, yes." He pauses. Then his eyes light up as he sets upon an example. "Take the Kennedy assassination. Was there a second shooter? A magic bullet? The physics of the situation don't line up, and yet all evidence suggests that Oswald acted alone. We'll never know what happened in the original timeline, but reality doesn't quite line up correctly when somebody has meddled with time; it's like a broken bone that doesn't quite heal."

"Wait, wait, wait," I say, clenching the steering wheel. "A time traveler killed John F. Kennedy?"

Rosey looks at me almost pityingly, as if he has to break an uncomfortable truth to a child. "What other evidence makes sense?"

"Does this mean we won't know whether or not we succeed on the case?" I ask.

"We might, if we know where to look," he responds. "But only if we spot something that doesn't fit with reality as we know it. A person who is alive when we swore they were dead, for example."

I sigh. "Well, let's not get ahead of ourselves. We have no clues. Not even you have found anything substantial yet."

"Well, the best step would be to talk to the man himself," Rosey remarks. "If we could get Captain Tomorrow out of whatever time-hole he's hiding in, we could get his resources to help us."

"You still really think he's out there somewhere, and not just on that slab in the morgue?"

"Definitely. When I talked to him, I told him he had died in our timeline. That probably rattled him—the guy who can see every possible future can't see the one that kills him" He pauses and stares into space for a moment, pondering.

"I he's hiding somewhere," he continues, "laying low lest the next leap is his last. Whatever's coming up is the biggest thing in his life, and it's the first time he really has no clue of what's going to happen or when it will hit him. If we could put together something to flush him out, we'd find out for sure."

"Something to flush him out?"

"Yeah," he says. "Back in the old days, I probably would have launched a missile at Los Angeles or kidnapped a loved one to get his attention. Make him choose between his own safety and the lives of innocents."

Things start clicking in my head. I wonder if this is how Rosey used to feel when he came up with a new type of death ray.

"Okay, I've got another client I need to meet in a couple of hours," I say. "I'll bring you home, but do you swear not to put one of those schemes you just mentioned into action?"

"I'm a new man, my dear." He holds up three fingers like he's giving a scout's pledge. "Five years in prison helped me realize it's easier to work with the law than go against it…no matter how inconceivably brilliant my latest plans might be."

"No giant robots? No kidnappings?"

"I don't have the resources to build a giant robot, and my little black book is far too out of date to stage a decent kidnapping."

I pull out of my parking spot and head toward the garage entrance. "Good enough. Let's go."

I don't have time to do anything but take Rosey at his word. Depending on how things go at my next meeting, the future might be much messier than either of us can imagine.

#9: RUNNING THE NUMBERS

*E*xcept for the genetically altered lizard-people, the sewers of Masters City are safer than people think. Unfortunately, the lizard-people want to see what I taste like, and they know the twists and turns better than I do.

"Pythagorasss..." The hiss comes from every direction and no direction, echoing through the tunnels around me. I had hoped their lifespans—or at least their memories—were shorter.

About seven years ago, I recruited the mutant lizards living under this city in an effort to destroy Paradigm. But things went badly, as they often do, and everyone's favorite crimson-clad hero convinced the lizard-people that I had been manipulating them all along—which I had been, but it was pretty rude of Paradigm to point that out. When the mutants turned against me, I teleported most of them off to a South American jungle where I would never have to deal with them again.

Seems I missed a few.

Each lizard-person stands about six and a half feet tall, full of green-scaled fury. The males run on all fours, bright frills out, while the females take a stealthier approach that makes them harder to spot until it's too late. At top speed, they can run about as fast as an Alaskan timber wolf.

My goggles get too much static from all the heavy metals in the pipes around me, but the shadows of my pursuers flicker on-screen from time to time. They finally catch up to me as I reach a junction where the path branches off in six directions. I stop in the dead center. The lizard-people shift to a two-legged stance, long claws out and ready.

The creatures wear no clothing and have no jewelry of any sort. Some bear tribal scars etched with fang and claw into their skin. The women crouch, claws ready and legs coiled to spring at a moment's notice. The men wield rotted baseball bats or old shopping cart rails as clubs. Their frills retract back against their necks as they close in. The largest of the females, the one directly in front of me, twitches her tail as she gets ready to strike.

"Pythagorasss," she hisses. "You dare to return."

Even if they didn't have me surrounded and offered me a head start, I wouldn't stand a chance running for much longer. I should have gotten Eva to lobby for some track time in the prison so I could keep my cardio up. "I assure you," I gasp, "I have a good explanation for all of this."

"No!" the leader shouts. "You ssspeak lies! You always ssspoke lies! And we are sssick of your deception!"

"I'm warning you," I say, reaching into my backpack. "Don't come any closer. You can give me a chance to explain, or—"

A red light starts blinking in the bottom corner of my glasses, warning me of danger from behind. One of the lizard-people broke ranks to attack the soft flesh of my exposed back. My fingers fumble for a split second, and I nearly have a heart attack. But then I find the metal cylinder in my backpack and push the red button on top of it.

With a crackle like metal in a microwave, the lizard-person disappears with a bright blue flash. Nothing but a whiff of ozone, itself barely detectable over the stench of the sewers, remains.

"Now," I say, drawing the black metal device out of its hiding place, "we can talk, or you can all meet a similar fate."

Ignoring my warning, the lizard-people charge forward with a collective howl. How did creatures without any capacity for reason ever expect me *not* to betray them?

In a foot race, they're faster than me. But with my finger already on the button, they could be the Human Bullet and they still wouldn't be able to stop me. I click the button five times in rapid succession, and each click zaps one of my attackers out of existence. The device grows too hot to hold after the last use, but it served its purpose. I drop the cylinder in the water. Steam rises and I hold my nose while moving on from the particularly pungent odor.

"Thank you, Captain Tomorrow."

A screwdriver, a fuse box, data retrieved from two time-displaced corpses...these are a few of my favorite things.

My glasses don't just duplicate Eagle Eye's multiple extraordinary fields of vision—they also store data. A few hours spent analyzing the information I gleaned from Captain Tomorrow's corpse allowed me to jury-rig a simple bit of weaponized time travel. It still has a long way to go, but the fact that the lizard-people aren't here now suggests that, if everything went according to my calculations, they'll re-materialize one hour into the future. By that time, I'll be long gone. If I forgot to carry the one, I just disintegrated the remaining members of their tribe. Either way, they won't bother me anymore.

The darkness of the sewers leaves me temporarily blinded once I slip my glasses off. Fortunately, I have another helpful gadget to aid me: a flashlight. Not everything in my arsenal needs to be some space-age wonder of mad science.

As I walk, I take a travel-sized packet of generic-brand acetylsalicylic acid, tear it open with my teeth, swallow the pills, and drop the wrapper into the brown-colored glop below me. I'm going to have a lot of headaches in the near future.

Among the numerous terms of my release is a temporary restriction on the purchase of over-the-counter drugs. I can only buy the travel-sized packs, and even then I can have no more than ten pills total on my person at any given time. It seems paranoid of the government to give a supposedly free man such stipulations. It becomes less paranoid, however, when I remind myself that I managed to hack my ankle monitor to send false coordinates to the authorities and jury rig a time machine in my spare time today.

So why am I in the sewers, violating Eva's request not to embark upon any crazy schemes, and risking life and limb against a group of revenge-crazed lizard monsters? Because I like to be prepared. And because I still have a job to do.

It takes another fifteen minutes of navigating the twists and turns, but eventually my path leads me to a brick wall with a circle of faded white spray paint. When I and I alone come within five feet, the circle lights up and the wall rotates. A recording of my own voice greets me as I step into the secret passage.

"Welcome back Roosevelt, you handsome devil."

I realize that behind my mania, lust for power, and occasional homicidal rage, I might have some serious narcissism issues to deal with someday. On the other hand, if I didn't call myself handsome, nobody would.

Fluorescent lights turn on automatically as the wall slides back into place behind me. The lab inside isn't anything to write home about—about a hundred square feet of stone walls and floors, with a web of copper wiring along the ceiling—but it serves its purpose. Masters City has absurdly spacious sewers thanks to pressure I applied when I was CEO of RP Industries, all so I could have a backup hideout lined with lead and surrounded by enough ambient noise that even x-ray vision and super-hearing wouldn't find it. Even so, I remind myself to be cautious. This place is for a single experiment only, and then I'm out of here. If someone catches me down here, I go back to prison. Then I don't get to solve this lovely puzzle.

It took me five years rotting in a cell to realize something that most people understand right away: playing the villain sucks. I wasted my talents and my intellect building death rays, mind control devices, killer robots, and a million other devices that, while technically impressive, never did anything more than provide a speed bump for my greatest enemies.

I guess the argument could be made that I simply aimed too high. I hear that out in New Mexico, somebody who calls herself La Chupacabra has made a solid career out of besting some vigilante known as the Sloth. But I happen to have the dignity to make a nemesis out of somebody with more brain cells than toes. I'd rather fail and wind up in prison a million times than have no pride in my work.

The thing is, it was never about getting rich or taking over the world or anything of the sort. I never even considered myself a villain, no matter how many laws I broke. It always boiled down to the rest of the world not understanding me. I looked up in the sky and saw dangerous creatures that lorded over the rest of us, and I tried to knock them down a peg.

There are only two kinds of superheroes: those who got their powers in some sort of accident and those who were born with them from the start. Everyone who has the will and the knowhow to put together their own super-suits and show off the strengths they earned through hard work winds up getting branded as a villain.

I saw my brain as a superpower. How could I not? I was working on a master's degree before I hit puberty. To get the world to appreciate that, I needed to do something nobody else could do. I needed to help them, and I saw throwing off the shadow of Paradigm, a relic of an era we didn't need anymore, was the way to do it. How can we ever fix anything in our own lives when men and women with those incredible powers fly around like gods and do everything for us?

Then, somewhere in prison, the realization set in. I had wasted more than a decade of my life on these stupid attempts to "free" the world. And in realizing that, I started to consider myself a real villain. My quest was supposed to be about helping humanity. And how did I try to help? By building orbital disintegration rays and power nullifiers. Where was the cure for cancer? Where was a manned space mission to Mars? I could have accomplished these things, but instead I spent my life playing fisticuffs with the same people I despised. While I blamed Paradigm for stopping muggers in Masters City instead of helping African villages to keep from starving to death, I committed that same sin—maybe even worse, since I had the vision and resources make those changes. Now I'm an ex-con with just the clothes on my back and a few pieces of jury-rigged tech.

But I'm older and wiser, so now I'll play the same game Paradigm and the others do. Solve a crime, bring a killer to justice, and people love you. Get some capital from that fame, and I'm back in business. I once built an entire multinational corporation from the patents I dreamed up as a teenager. Given some time, money, and a pardon from the government's scrutiny, I'll be back where I used to be. But this time, I'll do it better.

An old friend waits for me inside a dust-laden storage chest. It looks like plate mail and smells like mothballs, but it's still there, as sleek and chromed over as ever: my battle suit.

Well actually, it's my back-up battle suit—a prototype that predates the final version by about six months. But seeing as Paradigm ripped apart the original, this one will have to do.

Paradigm is a nuclear man. At full force his punches can have the impact of an atomic bomb. Fortunately for the world, he usually keeps himself tightly reigned in. If he really cut loose, he could easily level an entire city. I built the battle suit like a portable bomb shelter, capable of absorbing the force of any impact. As I strip down to my skivvies in preparation for climbing into the armor, I notice several significant dents in the metal from an early fight before I could finish the final version. Obviously, I hadn't yet perfected the impact resistance factor.

The suit adds almost two feet of height to my frame and weighs well over a ton. Once inside, I'm completely isolated except for what I see through my visor. I'm effectively in a sensory deprivation tank. Sensors on the exterior connect virtually to my brain, providing me with tactile senses as needed. After my initial battle with Paradigm, I made sure to modify those sensors to filter out extreme pain.

The test is simple: in order for any version of me to have killed Captain Tomorrow with existing technology, I would have had to control this engine of destruction to such a precise degree that I struck the man from behind with enough speed and power to puncture him in all the right places and not rip him in half.

I raise my arm and flick my wrist, drawing a foot-long titanium blade from a hidden sheath in the armor. Then I swing my arm and land a solid blow against the wall. The blade cuts through the stone like a rapier into an overly ripe watermelon, but the real item of interest is my hand. With the blade extending from behind the wrist and a foot outward, at even a tenth of my suit's full strength output, the blow leaves a fist-shaped imprint on the stone. I need to turn the power down even further.

I flick my other wrist and strike the wall again. It leaves a new cut and an indent, but this one is notably smaller than the first.

In theory, my battle suit has such fine muscle control that I can either pet a puppy or punch it into space, depending on my whim. I've never tested either aspect before, though...at least not on puppies. Superheroes I can deal with. The ASPCA, on the other hand, they're someone you do not want to cross.

I run some quick numbers through my head. I could decrease the power output of the suit far enough to stab Captain Tomorrow repeatedly without actually cutting through him or leaving those fist-shaped bruises, but it would require actively reigning myself in. The question is, why would I go through all that trouble? If I'm going to finally kill a superhero, why not just rip him in half?

The other question is a big one, too: even if future-me did choose this method to kill Captain Tomorrow, how did I get close enough to pull it off? He would have had to have his back to me at the start of the attack, and this suit is built for power, not stealth. Any cloaking devices I used to own are still property of the government, meaning I would have to steal them back somehow in order to access them. So either Captain Tomorrow trusted me enough to turn his back to me, something else had him distracted, or I'm on the wrong trail entirely.

Either I'm a murderer or I'm wrong. I don't find either possibility terribly comforting.

A blinking light on the bottom of my visor alerts me to an interesting fact. I take a deep breath and then started mumbling some calculations aloud for show. Nerve impulses in my brain tell my sensors to focus further, giving me sight beyond sight.

Somebody left a pair of footprints in the layer of dust behind me—somebody other than me. I have to be quick and decisive, just like in the old days.

I abruptly cut off my muttering and whirl around with speed that something as bulky as my battle suit shouldn't have. At the same time, I press down my middle and ring fingers against my palm. A jolt of electricity bursts from the suit, striking an invisible target.

A high-pitched wheeze greets my ears, letting me know I struck true. My victim stumbles backwards into the wall and slumps down. The familiar scent of ozone and singed flesh greets my nostrils, making me think of happier times.

The unwanted guest becomes visible as he loses consciousness. He wears an orange and white spandex suit with what could almost pass as a Mexican wrestling mask.

"Great," I mutter, pulling off my helmet. "They had Invisible Lad follow me."

So here I am, the reformed criminal, and I've just captured a superhero while raiding a hidden hideout filled with technology that, a court order prevents me from coming within one hundred yards of. What to do, what to do...

Well, I guess a little old-fashioned interrogation couldn't hurt. I'll just have to remember to lay off the death machines.

Probably.

#10: THE LAST TITAN

If Rosey thinks he had to deal with tight security, he should take a look at the 110-year old man. He's one client that I always need to take extra time to prepare for.

Parking outside a convenience store downtown, I let the top of the convertible down. The sun shines in my eyes but the breeze feels refreshing. I hear the squeak of a bicycle chain and adjust my rearview mirror to see Mei heading my way.

A little red in the face when she pulls up next to the driver's side of my car, she nonetheless seems quite pleased with herself. In fact, something seems very odd about her in general. If I didn't know any better, I'd say she looks almost happy.

"You're wearing makeup," I observe when I get a closer look at her.

"I think I maybe have a date after this," she says.

"A date?" I ask hopefully. "With a therapist?"

"No," she says with a sour expression. "Ew."

My ears burn as my face flushes. "That's not what I meant."

"Yeah, I know. I need to stop skipping sessions and talk about my inner angst and all that." She fishes into the pocket of her blue jeans, removes a small jewelry box, and hands it to me. "But if it's all the same to you, I'll just cross my fingers and hope I get to kiss somebody tonight."

I take the jewelry box from her and open it up. Two ruby stud earrings greet me.

"It looks like you have a date, too," Mei says.

"Hardly," I reply. "I'm meeting a client."

"Dr. Pythagoras?"

"No. An...older gentleman." I glance at myself in the mirror and put the earrings on. "Does Miss Destiny know you're giving these to me?"

"I'm sure she'll figure it out eventually," she says. "But it won't be because I tell her."

"Good girl." With the earrings on, I look back at Mei and find she's shifting her weight from one side of the bicycle to the next, practically dancing in anticipation. "Go enjoy your date, Mei."

"Well, it's not really...I mean, I'm working up to that." She starts off, but then stops a few feet from the car. "You're sure you don't need me for anything else? Or Miss Destiny?"

"Go have fun!" I order. If she's not going to keep her therapy appointments, she might as well at least enjoy a few minutes as a normal teen.

The facility looks like nothing more than a silver trailer sitting on the Great Plains. People would ignore it entirely if it wasn't for the fifteen-foot high electric fence and armed guards surrounding it on all sides. Photo ID and proper clearance get me past the perimeter, but I have to park my car a minimum of fifty yards from the building. Guards at the door confiscate all sharp objects and personal electronics, including my digital watch.

Inside, the ground floor is little more than a barracks with security monitors showing everything in each of the dozen subbasements—especially the single cell on the bottom level that houses their one prisoner.

The authorities feared Rosey might get his hands on something he could use—a paper clip or battery he could turn into a death ray. With this one, it's all about what he could do if he ever gets mad enough. Twelve levels of double-reinforced steel doors and electrified floors might not even slow him down.

An officer with a pair of stars on his collar meets me at the elevator and salutes. His hair looks older than his face – serving here for so long as made him go gray before his time.

"Been a while, Miss," he says. "What brings you in on such short notice?"

I stand straight and tall, matching him in stature. "Making sure my client is still being given his civil liberties, General Lucas."

The general wrinkles his nose. "So you couldn't give us at least a bit more notice? We're not running a country club here."

"You've had your mandatory twenty-four hours," I retort sharply. "You were at the hearing when those orders came down. Or don't you remember the fiasco we had on our hands last time?"

Lucas grumbles and punches a security code into the control panel of the elevator. The door slides open and he steps in first. I follow closely behind.

"Last time was an aberration, miss." His voice grows quieter and he says, almost to himself, "Just like Solomon Krenzler down there."

"The idea that my client is some sort of freak is exactly what led to that unfortunate incident, General," I say. "I would hope you learned from the experience."

The general harrumphs, his face reddening. "The men involved were punished accordingly and are no longer at this facility, Miss."

"Mm-hm."

He grunts and stands in awkward silence as the elevator takes us deeper underground. The monitor above the door shows me a compound that must resemble one of Rosey's wet dreams. It looks like I'm a century into the future; each immaculate white-walled, steel-floored subbasement teems with doctors and researchers, each pursuing answers to questions even Rosey doesn't know.

I think back to when I first started working on Rosey's case. At first, he didn't seem all that interested in having me on board. He spoke with me long enough to stick with his "a clone did it" story, but he never told me anything useful about himself or his actions. When I spoke with him in our private chamber, he barely responded to my questions, instead pausing to mutter to himself and draw invisible notes with his finger on the smooth metal table.

I needed his case. I had carved out a reputation as the woman who fixed people, and Roosevelt Pythagoras was going to be my crowning glory. The man who had forced a solar eclipse, who had held the state of California hostage...that man could be fixed. And I planned to do it.

On our fourth meeting, I brought a Rubik's cube for him to fiddle with while we spoke. I knew he could solve it in a matter of moments, so before I arrived at the prison, I took the colored stickers off and rearranged them, carefully altering the puzzle to make sure that no combination of twists and turns could solve it. That's when he smiled. That's when he actually started answering my questions and striving to rejoin society. That, I think, is the point where he fell a little bit in love with me.

That's Rosey—my Rosey. He's not happy unless he's got an impossible puzzle to solve.

One day, I found the cube missing from my purse. I reported it to the prison immediately, prompting what was probably a very uncomfortable search for Rosey. I hadn't learned to fully trust him. They never found it, and I'm still not exactly sure how he managed to hide it. Two weeks later, I found the Rubik's cube in my purse again—solved.

Rosey, stick this case through. Live on the chintzy settlement the government gave you, attend all your meetings, help find out what happened to Captain Tomorrow. Then you can move onto the big problems, like curing Solomon Krenzler.

The elevator reaches the bottom subbasement. General Lucas punches in another code to open the doors, followed by a voice prompt.

"Lucas, Robert B," he says in a slow, clear voice. "Authorization 051962 Green."

The door sticks a little bit, but slides open to allow us access. The long, sterile corridor features M-16s mounted near the ceiling on automated turrets, all leading up to a single locked door. Lucas leaves the elevator. I don't.

"Are you coming or not, Miss Corson?" he asks.

"Unless those guns are programmed to shoot lawyers, I think I can find my way to the end of the hallway." I gesture for him to return to the elevator. "I need privacy with my client. I don't need you."

He frowns deeply, but marches back into the lift. I step out as he steps in, and he salutes me sloppily as we pass.

"The room has security cameras, but the audio recorders will be left off as per court order," he tells me as I walk toward the door. "We wouldn't want anybody eavesdropping on your conversation with your pet monster, would we?"

I don't give him the dignity of a backwards glance. "That will be all, General."

Lucas punches a button in the elevator. The steel doors shut with a clang, leaving me alone and ready for my meeting.

Beyond the door at the far end of the corridor, Dr. Solomon Krenzler, a man who has seen two world wars and been at the heart of a nuclear explosion, sits in his wheelchair behind plate glass. The left half of his body is withered and dead—face twisted, nerves useless, limbs immobile except for the occasional twitch. If he loses his concentration, he drools out of the corner of his mouth. Some military personnel have already set me up with a chair facing the nearly unfurnished cell, as well as a clipboard, lined paper, and a felt-tipped pen for taking any notes I might need.

"Eva...why are you here?" Only half of his mouth moves as he speaks. One eye stays shut and the other seems empty as it stares at me.

"I'm your lawyer, remember?" I say defensively. "Considering the number of experiments performed down here, I need to make sure you've still got some civil rights."

"I didn't...hrm." He swallows loudly and clears his throat with a grumble. He leans forward in the chair, and the safety glass fogs from the breath coming out of one nostril. "I didn't ask you to come here."

"You didn't ask me to come last time, either, when the doctors here started cutting pieces off your body for their experiments," I remind him.

He runs his tongue over his lips. "They're not...not torturing me. They're...curing me."

I stand up. If I could touch the glass without bringing in a dozen guards, I'd pound on it right now. "You call this a cure? You've got total paralysis in half your limbs. Give them a few more months and your entire body will shut down."

"No transformations...not in two years now. It's progress."

"They're killing you. Slowly and painfully."

"If that's what it takes."

I sit back down. "You can't be satisfied with this life."

He leans back, breathing through his nose only. His left nostril makes a high-pitched wheezing noise only dogs should be able to hear. "I've lived for more than a century. Most of it miserable...hurm...I've been ready to die for a long time."

I touch my earring, pulling it partway out of the piercing and fiddling with the post.

Despite his age, Solomon shouldn't look like this. He was created in the same disaster that spawned Paradigm. Caught in the heart of a nuclear explosion, victim of atomic radiation gone wild...he's like Paradigm's dark twin. One became a living sun, imbued with strength and good looks and becoming the perfect man. The other remained a scientist who had secretly battled with depression for years. Occasionally, Solomon's emotions overpower his intellect. For most people in that situation, that means a suicide attempt. For him, he became a monster—a giant gorilla-like creature with no intellect and the desire for nothing more than destruction.

Solomon Krenzler is Titan. He brought atomic fire to the people. He gave America our Paradigm, but he's been paying the price ever since. He now has greasy strands of gray hair hanging out the side of his mostly-bald head, a body that's been practically turned into a paperweight, adult diapers, and a constant tremor in his right hand. He should be furious at the twist of fate that gave Paradigm perfection and left him with an eternal nightmare. Instead, he considers his current situation an improvement.

"You didn't come here...to check on me," Solomon says, twitching his head to the side in a repeated series of quick jerks.

"Of course I did." I pull my right earring out entirely and turn it over in my hands. "You're my client. Even if you don't want to get out of here, I still need to make sure you're treated humanely."

"Tried to kill myself once, you know. Hrk...no...not once...twelve times, I think."

"Recently?"

"Over the years. Titan kept stopping me. Gnrg...a gun to my head or poison in my system triggers the transformation...brings him out."

"Solomon, stories like this are why you should be in a hospital, not this prison."

"I've wanted to die for so...so...long," he says, barely acknowledging my words. "He keeps me alive. But I'm getting close now. They took my notes...used them correctly. Every cell that dies in me...it's hurting him, too. Maybe someday I'll die and not have to worry about him. So...so close now..."

"Solomon, Roosevelt Pythagoras is out of jail. It's big news. That's why I made the appointment. I've got more publicity and pull than I've had in a while. I could get you better living conditions."

"Pythagoras..." He frowns. "They really...released him?"

"They pardoned him," I correct. "He's innocent."

"No...I remember him...never innocent."

I press my fingers against the earring until the flesh turns white, then release some pressure. Solomon and Rosey have a complex history. Rosey has manipulated the Titan into fighting Paradigm before. But at the same time, he could never bring himself to lie to Solomon—he's one of Rosey's greatest heroes. Even in the old volcanic lab, in Rosey's bedroom, there were three posters of famous scientists: Einstein, Tesla, and Krenzler.

"I'm not going to get into his guilt or innocence with you," I say. "But Rosey's turned over a new leaf. He's a consultant with the police right now, investigating a case."

"Investigating...what?"

"The murder of Captain Tomorrow."

The news of one of the world's most famous superheroes dying doesn't even get a raised eyebrow from Solomon. What is it with these geniuses never acting even a little human?

"What's...in it for...mnrn...you?"

"I want to see if somebody like Rosey really can reform."

"You don't...believe in him?"

"I think he needs success early," I admit. "If he can't figure this out, I don't know what he'll do."

"What do you need...from me?"

"You're an expert on radiation, including quantum radiation. Rosey got some strange readings on two bodies—Captain Tomorrow's and...well, his."

For a moment, Solomon actually looks intrigued. "He traveled through time?"

"It looks that way" I answer. "Rosey thinks the dead Captain Tomorrow is from the near future. He thinks the present one is hiding for some reason. Is that possible?"

"Maybe. But Tomorrow's location...not the problem."

"What is the problem, then?"

He clears his throat and shifts in his chair. "How did they...both travel back? Tomorrow's technology...needs manual control. If time travel is a car...urgh...bad analogy..."

"Go on," I urge.

"There would need to be a driver," he continues, regaining his momentum. "No autopilot on Tomorrow's devices. Somebody...had to send them back for a reason."

"Now why didn't Rosey think of that?"

"You sure...he didn't?"

I lower my hand down to my gray skirt and tilt it so the palm faces downward. The earring spills out, dropping along my right leg on its way to the floor. I speak louder now, making sure that my voice covers up the slight skitter as it lands.

"Thanks for the help, Doc. It's kind of nice to see you using your big brain for something other than trying to kill yourself."

"Not trying...succeeding."

"You're not dead yet," I point out.

He closes his good eye and almost smiles. "Soon."

I look at the floor and kick at the earring, knocking it from the base of my chair to the corner of the room.

The jewelry is small enough for the movement to go unnoticed by the security cameras. My frustration is much less calculated, though. Solomon's desire to kill himself, extraneous circumstances or not, is my failure as a lawyer. Instead of leaving him to rot in a hole like this, I should have gotten him the mental care he needed. I don't care what kind of monster is inside him. It can be contained, but the process doesn't need to kill the man. Given the chance, I'd bet Rosey could figure something out.

"You know, if we find Captain Tomorrow's killer, it could be thanks to you," I tell Solomon. "This information you just gave me—it might be more useful than you think."

He just grunts and taps his shaky hand against the arm of his wheelchair.

"Right," I say, standing up and smoothing out my suit. "God forbid you admit to being useful. You just happened to secure America's place as a superpower, created the hero everybody loves so damned much, and Heaven knows what else. It's not all undone by one mistake, you know."

He starts humming to himself, tuning me out.

"Thank you for all your help, Solomon." I head for the door.

"Eva," he says just before I leave, "you dropped something."

"No I didn't," I say. "You're just imagining things, Doc."

The steel doors open automatically and then slide shut behind me, locking Solomon away in solitude again.

#11: THE PERFECT DEATHTRAP

Never underestimate the value of a well-constructed deathtrap.

Sure, when you've used a hypersonic harmonizer to knock out the spandex-clad vigilantes who've infiltrated your mutant death island in the Pacific, you could just shoot them. Modern sensibility even says you're dumb not to. But even with your greatest foe, sometimes you need something other than a quick, painless demise. That's where robotic sharks with laser cannon eyes, hidden pools of hydrochloric acid, and—if you've really given it some thought—an appropriate soundtrack all come in handy.

Of all my various schemes, my greatest success came about three years before I finally landed in jail, shortly after I figured out the secret behind nanotechnology. It's another example of something I could have used to better humanity, creating self-replicating machines to fight cancer instead of the forces of do-goodery, but I was what I was.

Instead of releasing the technology to the public or even letting the researchers at my own corporation examine it, I put together a set of mind-controlling nanomachines. Injected through a serum, the intelligent machines went directly for the brain, where they multiplied and rewrote synapses, effectively reprogramming anybody to follow my orders.

I hit eight members of the League of Liberty. Using them, I captured Paradigm. I could have had his friends finish him off, but I opted for a deathtrap instead.

I shackled the weakened Paradigm to the wall of a steel bunker and targeted him with a blast of focused radiation designed to rapidly age his nuclear-powered core—essentially, a prototype of the entropy ray that I've had bouncing around in my head ever since I was a kid on the playground. By my calculations, the process had a 50% chance of burning out his powers entirely, rendering him nothing but a mere mortal, and a 50% chance of causing a nuclear explosion that would envelope the entire island. Given the dangers, I watched the whole thing remotely from my corporate office in Masters City.

Then Paradigm managed to vibrate his body at super-fast speeds, melting through his titanium restraints and boring through the bunker wall. He flew the mind-controlled heroes into low-Earth orbit, burning out the nanomachines and saving the day. I still wonder if he managed to calculate the right height to destroy the nanomachines without harming his friends or if he just got lucky.

Yes, maybe I should have killed Paradigm when I had the chance. But I always liked the idea of dealing the damage when I was well away from the scene. First, it made it much easier to have an alibi. No, officer, I couldn't have murdered all those superheroes; I was in a board meeting all day. Second, with somebody as powerful as Paradigm, I never knew if he was feigning helplessness or not. If I got in range to shoot him, he could have surprised me by charging at super speed and punching me into the next county.

Even in failure, though, I found success. The experience wound up tearing apart the League of Liberty from the inside. Paradigm and the others remained allies, even rebuilding their friendships after a time, but the League dissolved shortly afterwards, never fully able to trust each other again. I assume there was already inherent mistrust behind the scenes, with my scheme only serving as a trigger to an inevitable schism. Still, the experience reminded me that the difference between success and failure is often only a matter of perspective.

Most importantly, putting Paradigm through a long elaborate death trap gave me a chance to really examine his strengths and weaknesses in ways I couldn't when I was dealing with him in punching range. I didn't know he could move his body in such a way as to create a sympathetic resonance with certain metals, and now I do. While I had him unconscious, my capture-bots ran a battery of tests on his body, giving me a fascinating breakdown of physical data that I never had before. Nothing could stop me from learning.

Of course, now I'm stuck as a reformed villain who has just captured a superhero. If I let him go, he reports back to the authorities about my hidden lab and the tests I was running, and I wind up back in jail because it looks like I'm gearing up for another run at world domination. If I dispose of him, the other heroes he's been in contact with will know who killed him. I'm in trouble either way, and I have neither the time nor the resources to set up a good deathtrap.

I slip on my goggles and examine Invisible Lad's motionless body. His pulse rate is steady and his vitals are fine. I estimated correctly and used just enough electricity to knock him out while not flash-frying his nervous system. That's all those years of not killing people paying off.

I could just tell him the truth, but what are the odds he'll believe me? I could scamper away and hope I outrun him, but then he'll still report back to whomever else he's working with. And I can't collect my thoughts properly because of the incessant dripping and the odious smell of Masters City's collective liquid waste just outside my lab.

I do what I can to assert control over the situation. Before he wakes up, I'm out of my battle suit and back into my civilian clothes. I sling my backpack over my shoulder and slouch against a wall to appear as casual and nonthreatening as possible.

"Pyth...Pythagoras..." he murmurs as he comes to.

"I'm unarmed." I say. "We're on the same side...I hope."

"That why'd you light me up like a Christmas tree, bub?"

"You startled me," I defend, "and I'm already on edge. Assuming you've been following me for a while now, I'm guessing you spotted the giant lizard-men out to eat me."

He takes a fighting stance. "The ones you disintegrated? Yeah, I noticed that."

I groan. We're going to wind up doing this the hard way, which means lots of aches and pains for me in the morning. "I didn't disintegrate them—just displaced them. In another thirty-three minutes or so, they'll be back...and I hope to be gone by then."

"Oh, you'll be gone, all right, bub." He takes pains to sound rugged so I don't see him as that annoying little sidekick I remember. "I've got a prison cell all warmed up for you."

"This looks bad, but I've got a good explanation," I say, trying to sound amicable. "It all relates to Captain Tomorrow's death. Now that I've got the data I need, I'm willing to turn all this old tech in to the supers of the city so they can use it however they feel is best. I'm giving you a gift, Invisible Lad. You see—"

"That's Invisible Man now, bub," the kid snaps. "I've changed, even if you haven't."

I can't help but quip at that. "Invisible Man? Isn't that copyrighted by some movie studio?"

"Shut up!"

He lunges forward and I quickstep backwards. My hand goes for the stun gun, but a clap of thunder and a flash of red light stop us before we begin.

"Enough!" comes a woman's voice. I recognize it immediately. So does Invisible Lad.

"Don't fret yourself, Miss Destiny," he says. "I can take this joker down mano a mano."

"He said after fifteen minutes of lying unconscious on the floor," I jab back.

"Neither of you will fight," Miss Destiny commands. "I sent you to investigate, Invisible Man, not to start a battle. If I had known your stealth would not suffice, I would have sent another."

He bristles and clenches his fists, but doesn't respond. I take careful note of the irritation in Miss Destiny's tone and the way her ally looks like he's about to hit her. It seems all is not well in the superheroing world.

With her assistant properly chided, Miss Destiny turns her attention to me.

"Invisible Man was to check back with me periodically via radio signal," she explains. "I teleported to his location when he did not respond." She looks significantly at the suit of armor and the rest of my boxes and crates. "I see you have been busy."

Do what Eva would want, I remind myself. *Stick to the script.* "I just got here, and then only to test a theory I have about Captain Tomorrow's death. You see, I set this secret lab up years ago as a fallback location should my clone destroy my first base of operations."

"And?"

"I needed to figure out what kind of force would have been necessary to kill Captain Tomorrow," I continue. "The battle suit could theoretically have done it, which is why I'm turning it over to you and whatever authorities you call in to deal with this. It should be disposed of immediately, just in case."

She looks very carefully at the armor. "Is it fully functional?"

"Close enough. I wouldn't trust it to go toe to toe with Paradigm, but it could kill almost anybody else."

Miss Destiny frowns and folds her arms. "Very well, then."

"You're not really buying this load, are you?" Invisible Lad interjects.

"He attacked after he discovered you, did he not?"

Invisible Lad says nothing. Admitting that would be admitting that the master of stealth wasn't so stealthy after all.

"I choose to trust you, Dr. Pythagoras. After all, you are an innocent man, are you not?"

"Of course," I reply with as affable a smile as I can muster.

She stares at me as though she can see the lies that are etched into my soul. "Very well. It has been a pleasure to work with you so far, Dr. Pythagoras, and I appreciate the civil service you are performing by leaving this equipment to the proper authorities. But for right now, it is best if you return home."

"Well yes, I—"

Before I can finish my sentence, she waves her hands and snaps her fingers. The lab melts away and I feel the not-so-unfamiliar sensation of reality folding in on itself. I blink, and when my eyes open I'm sitting on the stained yellow couch in my furlough apartment. My head spins, but I don't have time to lie down and rest. My cell phone is ringing.

"Hello?" My voice sounds like I'm going to be sick. I clear my throat in an attempt to rectify that.

"Rosey, where have you been?" Eva asks.

"Somewhere with really bad reception." There's something loud in the background on her end. "I thought you were visiting with a client. Where are you?"

"I'm at the end of the whole damned world!"

Now that my head's cleared up, I realize she's shouting to get heard over the din around her. "What are you talking about?"

"Remember Titan?"

Ah...the good Dr. Krenzler. You never realized how incredible the monster inside you truly was. "Of course I do."

"Well, as of five minutes ago he broke out of the facility holding him," she shouts. "He's on the loose, Rosey. Find a way to get down here if you can. That distraction to flush out Captain Tomorrow is here."

"Right." I respond. "I'll meet you at the scene."

I put the phone down and stand up. That's when I notice it—my stun gun is gone, left behind in Miss Destiny's teleportation spell. How closely has she been watching me, and what is her magic really capable of?

A rummage through my backpack reveals that my other tech is still there. I briefly consider returning to the sewers and taking a chance to grab my battle suit before the authorities can get hold of it. It would turn me from a skinny nerd into a nigh-invulnerable being capable of standing toe to toe with almost anybody.

I sigh and shake my head, then start digging through my backpack. No…not yet. Better let the "real" superheroes take care of things for now.

#12: DAMAGE REPORT

The whole world is about to end. Where are all the superheroes?

I left my car a mile back after the military chased Titan off the highway and into the grasslands. They move in two waves: the manned vehicles that ride ahead to evacuate roads and farms in the monster's path, and remote-controlled tanks and aircraft designed by the former League of Liberty.

I've been following on foot for about half an hour now, which is a lot more impressive than it sounds. No one can effectively chase an atomic monster off-road in a pair of high heels. But I need to keep moving no matter what, because I need to know which supers show up on the scene. Even with the League of Liberty disbanded, a handful of threats can bring them all together. A rampaging Titan is one of them.

I pull off my high heels and pick up the pace. Some blisters and ruined nylons will be a small price to pay if this disaster bears fruit.

Somebody grabs my arm and I whirl around instinctively to smack him. I stop myself just in time to avoid pummeling the suddenly-there Rosey, who has already flinched in anticipation of the incoming blow.

"Rosey, where the heck did you come from?"

He points to a cell phone-sized clipped on his belt. "I dug some old tools out of storage."

"What storage?" I yell to get over the sound of nearby gunfire. "Most of your tech was confiscated. You didn't steal anything, did you?"

"No of course not." He hesitates, and I can see him trying to get the story straight in his head. "Miss Destiny even gave me permission to use the stuff I have here."

I narrow my eyes in suspicion, but any interrogations has to wait. A helicopter fires a series of missiles, and the heat from the resulting fireball feels like an instant sunburn. Titan, in the center of that inferno, probably thinks it tickles.

"Any supers on the scene yet?" Rosey shouts.

"No," I reply. "Looks like they're off hiding somewhere."

"Don't worry, they'll be here any second now. Come on...we should get a little closer to the action." He offers me his hand, too timid to just grab my arm again.

"This is going to suck, isn't it?" I reluctantly take Rosey's hand, and he presses a button on his belt. The next few seconds confirm my suspicions.

Reality folds around us and belches us out a few dozen yards from the raging battle. He must have tried explaining to me how his teleportation devices work a dozen times, but I've never understood it. All I know is it makes my stomach churn and gives me a nosebleed.

No sooner are we back in the physical world than we both drop to our hands and knees as a tremor from Titan's stomping foot throws us off balance. Rosey digs into his backpack for his glasses so he can get a closer look at Titan in action. I tilt my head back and pinch the bridge of my nose, cursing under my breath all the while.

As Titan, Solomon stands ten feet tall with gray skin and yellow eyes. He has at least a half-ton of muscle on that frame, all hiding under matted black hair that's not quite thick enough to be considered fur. His brilliant mind of is all but gone, leaving him incapable of speech above guttural growls and roars. The only thing left of his brain is an id that knows nothing but hatred—Solomon's own grudge against himself transformed and focused outward against the rest of the world.

Another barrage of machinegun fire rattles off Titan's impenetrable hide. The stink of gunpowder hanging in the air burns my nose and makes my eyes water. Titan charges the tank firing at him. He places a palm against the cannon-sized barrel, stopping the shells before they can clear the opening. Jammed, the barrel explodes, knocking Titan on his back but also ruining the tank. The gray behemoth gets up within a few seconds. The tank remains nonfunctional, smoke billowing from its top.

Thankfully, the government realized long ago that pitting real soldiers against the monster was just throwing lives away. Before Rosey broke up the League of Liberty, the smartest of the supers assembled to create this remote arsenal. The unmanned tanks can't adjust as well as a human brain can, but they serve their purpose of keeping him contained, getting him focused on tearing apart machines instead of stomping cities flat.

Besides, the machines are only there as a stalling tactic until some supers show up to save the day. So where are they?

A helicopter flies by and keeps the heat on. Titan crouches down, leaps into the sky as easily as a child playing hopscotch, and grabs the front nose of the aircraft. The added weight sends it spinning out of control. They both hit the ground, and the explosion leaves a lingering high-pitched squeal in my head.

"Do you see something odd here?" Even though he's yelling, I can barely hear Rosey over the surrounding fury.

"You mean besides the fact that a giant rampaging monster belongs in Tokyo and not the American heartland?"

"Titan's not himself." Rosey adjusts his glasses, focusing solely on the raging beast. "He's feeling this stuff. It's hurting him a little. He should be getting stronger as the battle goes on, but instead he's slowing down."

Panting now, Titan raises his fists above his head and slams them against the ground. A fissure opens, dragging a tank under the earth. Rosey and I get to our feet and run for sturdier ground lest we join it.

"So what does that mean?" I ask, my mouth dry. "We might not need the supers to finish the job?"

"No such luck," Rosey replies. "But it's odd. Solomon Krenzler who gets old and weak, not Titan."

I grab Rosey by the arm. Unlike me, his first instinct is not to lash out. He just turns and looks at me with those small dark eyes of his.

"I visited Solomon earlier today," I say.

Rosey raises an eyebrow.

"Don't give me that," I continue. "I was doing my job. He's stuck in that facility and they've been trying to kill Titan off—burn out the cells in his body that cause the transformation."

"And?"

"And Solomon was practically a vegetable, nearly paralyzed and barely able to wipe the drool off his own chin."

"They must have found a way to burn out the radiation in his cells," says Rosey, adding the variables together. "If Titan's like a cancer, they're administering chemotherapy. But unlike a cancer patient, Dr. Krenzler can't be without his illness. They've shared the same body since World War II...killing Titan means killing Krenzler. But whatever cure they're giving him, Titan's still not weak enough to get dropped by these tin cans."

"No need to worry about that now," I say, pointing over Rosey's shoulder and toward the horizon. "The big gun has finally arrived."

We both stop paying attention to the battle with Titan and turn our attention to the red blur zipping through the clouds. Paradigm doesn't go right for the monster, though. He stops near us first, hovering in the air above our heads with his arms crossed and his cape flapping in the breeze.

"Hey big guy," I shout. "The battle's over there. We're just innocent bystanders."

I can't see his face clearly, but I think he's frowning as he flies toward Titan.

"I don't think he's happy with us being here," I say.

"I don't think he's ever happy," Rosey responds. "For a guy who can fly around the Earth and survive in deep space, he never seems to have any fun doing it."

"Maybe he just never smiled around you because he was too busy punching you in the head."

Rosey lets my comment go with a dismissive wave, then points to Paradigm. "Here comes the pre-battle banter. Paradigm will try to talk Titan down. Something along the lines of, 'I know you're in there, Dr. Krenzler. We don't have to do this.'"

"Will it work?"

"Probably not," he says, "but that's what the good guys always do. Titan will punch him around for a bit, but the other supers will get here soon enough to turn the tide."

"Do you think the others might include Captain Tomorrow?" I ask hopefully.

Rosey doesn't seem to hear me—he keeps his focus locked on the confrontation ahead of us.

Titan turns his attention to the flattened steel sheet that was once the armored body of a tank. Then he finally takes notice of Paradigm. The American marvel floats in the air a few yards in front of his old foe, arms folded and wearing the same dour expression he had when he saw us.

The silent showdown lasts a few seconds, during which time I keep waiting for Paradigm to start talking. Instead, he unfolds his arms, clenches both of his hands into fists, and flies toward Titan at full speed. The monster tries to react, but he's a step too slow. The force of Paradigm's punch sounds like another bomb going off. With a howl Titan finds himself knocked several hundred yards backwards. Paradigm doesn't even wait for him to land—he starts flying after him, raining down more blows on his foe in midair.

"Wait…that's not right," Rosey says. "He didn't even give him a chance to talk."

"Titan doesn't speak words. Maybe Paradigm's finally realized that."

"No. He's not acting like himself." Rosey holds his hand out for me to take it again.

"More teleporting?" I groan.

"We need to keep close to the battle and see what's happening," Rosey answers. "Are you coming or not?"

I sigh and place my hand in his. The things I do for my clients.

Upon landing closer to the rapidly moving battle, we hear a howl that sounds like a dying wolf. Titan reels from Paradigm's punches. His simple mind isn't used to feeling pain and panic.

"Paradigm's changed since I've been locked up," Rosey says.

"It's hard to say for sure," I respond. "No one really knows what goes on in inside his head. Most folks never see him except in news reports, and even then it's only at a distance."

Titan lands a punch that knocks Paradigm backwards. Then he rips a chunk of rock out of the ground and throws it at his foe, but Paradigm has already recovered. Easily dodging the projectile, he flies in to renew his attack.

"He's got a killer instinct he didn't have before," Rosey says. "Or maybe it's just Titan that brings that out in him."

"Why Titan?" I ask. "I thought you were his arch-nemesis."

Rosey winces in sympathy as Paradigm connects with a haymaker to Titan's jaw. Then he responds to me by shaking his head. "I took my shots at him long after he'd already been on the scene. Titan was there from the beginning, like his twisted twin. And I think Paradigm has always had a bit of a grudge against him because Titan is the only thing on this planet that's been capable of really hurting him without having to rely on some gadgetry to level the playing field."

The monster howls again and connects with a right hook to Paradigm's nose. A trickle of blood runs down his chin.

"But Titan's not a bad guy deep inside," I say. "Deep down, he's always been Solomon Krenzler, a guy who worked with Paradigm on the Manhattan Project."

"I don't know what role Paradigm had in that project, but I doubt he was a scientist," Rosey says, always quick to deny his foe that distinction. "He's never had an appreciation for people with brains." He reaches into his pocket and produces a pair of thick blue earplugs. "Here…put these in."

"Why?" Even as I ask the question, I take the earplugs from him.

"I've never fought Titan hand to hand, but I've studied his tactics. He's getting hurt here, which means he's about to change things up." Rosey puts in some earplugs of his own and adds in a loud voice, "You'd better hurry."

I put in the earplugs and the world goes quiet, like I'm in a swimming pool and the fight is going on all the way at the other end.

Titan leaps into the air, attempting to get himself some distance from his attacker. Paradigm follows, and that turns out to be a mistake. The monster spreads his arms wide and claps his hands together as hard as he can. It's a normal person's loudest handclap multiplied a million times by Titan's immense strength. The result is like a fleet of jets all hitting the speed of sound at once. Even with the benefit of the earplugs, I close my eyes and hold my hands over my head. When I open my eyes again, I'm on my knees. Rosey isn't much better, practically face-down in the dirt and panting. He gets up quicker than I do, but I attribute that to the fact that he's used to getting the stuffing kicked out of him by supers.

The dust and debris kicked up by Titan's thunderclap leaves us blinded for a moment. I squint my eyes against the bits of dirt and grass that suddenly become tiny knives in the whirlwind of chaos. By the time we can see clearly again, the fight seems to have turned against Paradigm. Super-hearing is probably great until you're right next to a sonic boom.

Now Paradigm's pretty boy image is mussed up, his cape is torn, and his ears are bleeding. Titan pins him down with one massive hand and starts hitting him like he's a drum set. I cast a glance over toward Rosey. If he's concerned about Paradigm's peril, he doesn't show it—his face keeps the same clinical calm he has when he's talking about a science experiment.

Rosey moves his lips, but I can't hear him with the earplugs in. I take one of them out and cup a hand to my ear. Taking my cue, he repeats himself.

"Even weakened, Titan's close to a match for Paradigm," he says. "So where are the other heroes? They should help their buddy out."

The question becomes moot as the Paradigm catches Titan's incoming fist in both his hands. With a grunt and then a shout, he pushes the monster backwards. Stunned that his power isn't enough to win the day, Titan roars and pounds his chest. He spreads his arms out for another thunderclap, but Paradigm finally puts his speed to good use, zooming in close to the monster and catching his hands as they come together, preventing the impact that stunned him before. Then he flies upward, taking Titan off the ground and negating some of his strength advantage.

Still showing some fight, Titan gives Paradigm a headbutt, knocking him out of the sky. But Paradigm lands on his feet, bends his knees, and uses the momentum to carry him into his next blow. He springs upward as Titan comes down, raising his fist and delivering a solid blow to Titan's jaw. The falling monster goes hurtling back into the sky, then goes limp as it hits the ground a dozen yards away.

"Maybe Paradigm doesn't need the help after all," I say.

"Oh, he can hold his own, sure enough" Rosey grudgingly agrees. "But how's he going to put the big guy down? He's going to need help to subdue him, unless…"

Rosey's voice trails off as he continues to watch the battle. Standard procedure for Paradigm at this point would be to grab some of the steel from the surrounding wreckage, bend it to serve as makeshift manacles for the monster, and hope it holds. But he doesn't seem willing to end the fight there. He pauses long enough for the monster that was my client to get back up on his hands and knees. Then he delivers another head shot to knock Titan back down.

"What's he doing?" I ask Rosey.

Rosey gives a thousand-yard stare. He doesn't have an answer.

Titan's roars go from enraged to frightened, and then from frightened to pathetic. Every time the monster gets up, it's a little slower. And each time, the punch that knocks him down comes faster.

"He's going to kill him!" I start running, and Rosey follows my lead.

"He must not realize that Titan's weakened." Rosey starts waving his arms over his head as he runs. "Hey! Hey, stop!"

"Get back!" Paradigm yells. "The fight's not done yet."

"Of course it is," I shout. "You've already won!"

Paradigm shakes his head. With Titan still down from the last punch, he slams his fists together, creating a thunderclap of his own. The force knocks both Rosey and I reeling. I land on my back and my vision stays blurred for a bit. My ears shut off, leaving nothing but a loud buzzing in my head as my brain tries to protect me from any more sound.

When we both regain some semblance of hearing and awareness, the two combatants are nowhere to be found.

"Where'd they go?" I ask. "Did we black out?"

"No," Rosey groans. "Look, up in the sky."

Titan himself is just a speck at first, and Paradigm is even smaller. The two get bigger fast. Paradigm flies downward at breakneck speed, his arms wrapped firmly around Titan's waist. Titan himself doesn't seem to have any more resistance to offer.

"What's he doing…he's going to kill Solomon!"

"Never mind that," Rosey says. "He's going to kill us if we're too close to the point of impact. Run!"

With my stockings torn and my feet blistered, I won't be able to make it very far at all. So I do something that I instantly regret: I throw my arms around Rosey, pull him close to me, and hit the red button on his belt. We disappear just before Paradigm hits earth like a falling meteor.

We land in a heap, with Rosey on the bottom and my foot in his face. Compared to Titan, we got the better of it.

The crater caused by the impact is at least twenty feet deep. A cloud of thick brown dust still covers the area. Paradigm hovers above it, face bruised and costume tattered. Tanks and jeeps race toward the scene. I hear shouts of victory as people hail Paradigm as their hero once again.

Rosey and I cast our eyes toward the bottom of the crater, where Titan's broken body lies. His face is mangled almost beyond recognition and his limbs are twisted. He starts to shed the coarse hair that covers his body and begins to shrink, muscle melting away into evaporating liquid as he goes from a ten-foot-tall hulk of a creature to a ninety-eight pound crippled man. From the distance we're at, we can't tell if Solomon is even breathing.

"Maybe Paradigm was trying to knock Titan unconscious," I say to Rosey. "KOing him turns him back into Solomon, right?"

Rosey doesn't move except to shake his head. "No…something's different. He's different. I've been in jail for too long, and now all the rules have changed."

#13: AFTERSHOCK

I never considered my nemesis a coward, but now I have to wonder. Knowing that we saw what we saw, he can't seem to get away from this place quickly enough.

He flies away in a crimson blur, and I feel surprisingly small. I miss the days when we used to banter back and forth, me polishing up my smug snake smile as I delivered thinly veiled threats and him cliché-ing me to death. Now he has nothing to say, and that makes him more dangerous than ever. The broken monster in the crater serves as proof that he might drop a boulder on me from orbit if I ever step too far out of line.

"What now?" Eva asks. She has dried blood smeared across her face, and her business attire has become a shredded collection of dirt and rags. I imagine I don't look any better.

"You should tend to your client," I respond. "Make sure he's still alive."

We don't have much time to waste—not with jeeps and choppers converging in on the battle site. Eva puts a hand on my shoulder. I tap the red button on the teleporter, but nothing happens. I pull the black box off its belt clip to see what's wrong. The back falls off, revealing its fried circuitry.

"What happened?" Eva inquires.

"The shockwave from the battle must have damaged my device." I put the broken machine in the rear pouch of my backpack.

No sense in letting spare parts go to waste. "We'll have to get back to the scene on foot."

Eva groans and says the same thing I'm thinking right now. "That's easier said than done."

Walking around with internal bleeding and mild fractures reminds me of the old days, but not in a good way. My aching body keeps telling me it doesn't want to move anymore, that with the next step my ankle will buckle and my legs will give out. The fact that we're walking back toward a combat zone doesn't help. Physically, it's more difficult to travel thanks to the fact that a once-flat expanse has been reduced to a pock-marked wasteland. We navigate around spots where the force of the battle thrust the ground upwards like a cresting wave on the ocean. We hop over the fissure created when Titan pounded his fists against the earth, idly looking into the crevice and wondering how deep it goes. The battle's finale left a series of concentric circles for several dozen yards, each going a little deeper until they reach the bottom of the crater. There, paramedics load a naked Dr. Krenzler onto a stretcher.

Psychologically, each step serves as a reminder of how fragile we both are. Eva's probably used to the helpless feeling in a world where men can fly through the sun and mutants live in the sewers. I spent most of my adult life striving to put myself on the level of those gods, building machines that could help me walk through a nuclear explosion and survive the Earth's molten core if need be. But when my tech is broken, when my defenses finally get torn down, I am very weak and very mortal.

We split up as we get close to the perimeter established by the incoming troops. Eva can bluff her way in thanks to her ability to bark orders as effectively as any general. She'll make it seem like she belongs on the scene when in reality protocol demands keeping her away until Krenzler is secured. I, on the other hand, couldn't get in the middle of things if I was a five-star general. Even if I'm technically cleared of my past crimes, anybody who looks at me still sees the cackling maniac who once demanded a trillion-dollar ransom from the United Nations. So while Eva storms onto the scene,

I slink around the edges, hiding behind the ample camouflage made available by upturned soil, downed trees, and shattered boulders.

Fortunately, there are more soldiers and paramedics on the scene than necessary. Most of the force that had been evacuating the area doubled back with news of Paradigm's arrival on the scene. With so many people and only one man to take back into custody, that means a lot of milling about and looking important with nothing substantial to do. Now that the fight has provided me with some cover, I can sneak up right behind one of those idle soldiers.

I look for the highest-ranking officer whose clothes I can wear. A major or colonel would be nice, but I'm stuck with a Lieutenant, Second Class. I shimmy on my belly behind the remnants of a broken tank, wait until I see his back, and then pop out of hiding. A fast chop to the neck stuns him. Then my left arm locks around his throat, just below the Adam's apple. The soldier gurgles as I pull him back behind cover. He loses consciousness in a matter of seconds, never having seen his assailant.

I sigh as I remember my promise not to commit more crimes. Then again, a clever lawyer like Eva would argue that this counts as vigilante action—technically illegal, but ultimately serving the side of law and order. Sort of like when Invisible Lad knocked out my henchmen and infiltrated my moon base. That was the last time I used non-robotic minions, which was just as well—getting them healthcare benefits was unbelievably difficult.

I emerge from hiding in the soldier's outfit and my pair of special glasses. I take a bit of extra time to make sure my own clothing and backpack are well away from the scene of the crime before making my way to the truck containing Dr. Krenzler.

Stand tall and look mean, Roosevelt, I tell myself. *You'll wind up back in jail if you screw this up.*

A set of solid steel manacles with no key restrains Krenzler's arms. When he gets back to his prison, they'll need a cutting torch to get those things off him. Similar fetters bind his legs. None of that matters—if he transforms again, he'll tear apart the restraints like wet tissue paper. But I don't think he has another transformation in him for a while yet…not with the beating Paradigm just gave him.

"We've got him stabilized," the officer says. "You're not needed."

I stand stiff and force my face into a hard grimace as I look straight into the soldier's face. His eyes stare back at me without a hint of recognition, and I have to struggle to keep myself from smiling at the apparent success of my makeshift disguise. People don't really recognize faces—they recognize context. Take me out of a laboratory, keep me from laughing maniacally, and I can be a perfect chameleon.

"I need to talk to the prisoner alone," I shout over the noise of engines and rotor blades.

"No one talks to him until we get him back under lock and key. Those are the orders from General Lucas."

"You really think Lucas is the one calling orders on this one, boy?" I bark. "We're dealing with something way over his head."

"Then you bring me some proper orders from a ranking officer and I'll think about it," he snaps. "Until then, you don't get to say word one to him."

He finishes loading Krenzler into the medical van. The officer climbs in, and I jump in after him.

"Hey, what the heck are you—"

A solid punch to the gut dazes him, and then a pinch to the right nerves puts him down for a few minutes. I turn and slam the doors of the ambulance. I don't notice that I can't move my right thumb until I'm standing by the stretcher that holds Krenzler. I know where to hit people to take them out, but I'm still inexperienced enough to punch them with my thumb on the inside of my fist. I guess I have a long way to go before I become a competent vigilante.

Krenzler's tongue hangs halfway out of his mouth and his eyelids flutter as I shine a flashlight from a nearby supply case into his face. Once he's got some semblance of awareness back, he gasps as he sees past my disguise.

Good. He recognizes me, and he remembers he doesn't like me. If he can speak, I'll consider that a bonus.

He moans, then spouts random syllables as he tries to bridge the gap between his brain and his larynx. Half of his face responds; the other half is already dead.

"Unn...ugnh...you..."

"Yes Dr. Krenzler. Me."

"Trying....ta...ta...to make me transform again."

"Not at all. You don't answer questions so well when you're big and gray, and I don't have the time to properly interrogate you."

"You...you'll get caught here. You'll go b-back to jail."

"Maybe they'll allow us to share a cell. In the meanwhile, why don't you tell me what set you off, Dr. Krenzler?"

"Rngh...ask your girlfriend."

"What's that supposed to mean?"

"Eva. Dropped an earring near my cell. Next thing I know...explosion. Could have killed me. Should have, this time."

My eyes shift from side to side as I try to put things together. I never told Eva where any of my hidden labs were. Even if I did, my inventions never included explosive fashion accessories.

"Titan saved you, like he always does," I inform him.

"Not saved," he retorts. "Cursed."

"It's not a curse—it's preservation. Somebody with your emotional issues, doctor, would have put a gun to his head and pulled the trigger long ago. Thankfully, Titan always stops you from doing something stupid."

"Not stupid. I just want to be free."

"Freedom from life isn't real freedom. Imagine what you could have done for this world if you had just accepted who you are."

"Or what you...could have done."

I give a wry smirk. "Believe me, doctor, I've had plenty of time to consider that. But back to the issue at hand. Even if Eva did cause the explosion, she would have known it would just force you to transform."

His breathing becomes labored and he moans.

"If you really want to die, you should consider asking Paradigm," I tell him. "He nearly made that wish come true for you.

With Titan weakened by whatever treatment they've given you, he nearly beat you to death."

"Would have been for the best."

"You're so eager to die that you don't even wonder why the man who hasn't taken a life since 1954 suddenly comes close to committing murder?"

"He didn't know my condition. Didn't know it affected Titan."

"Wrong. I know you can remember what happened during your transformations, even if your mind is stuck somewhere deep inside that monster's body. Paradigm had Titan beaten, but he kept going full force. He didn't care whether you lived or died."

"He almost...almost did me a favor."

"Whether he was giving you what you wanted or not, it was something he never used to even consider. No matter how many times you two fought, he always remembered there was a man inside."

"Just like you always knew there was a monster...to manipulate on the outside."

I take a sharp suck of air at the barb. Yes, I always knew what Dr. Krenzler was capable of. He was the only mortal on Earth who could break Paradigm's jaw with one solid punch. And while Krenzler could see through any scheme I might think up, Titan's mind was simple and bestial enough to manipulate. In my darker moments, consumed with the idea of finally winning this never-ending battle, I stirred up that irradiated hornet's nest and pointed it at my enemies. It's about the only thing I've ever done that I knew was wrong at the time. Considering what Dr. Krenzler has given to humanity during his lifetime, I should have had more respect for the man. But I can't dwell on the past right now. I don't have the time.

"Why was Eva even there?" I ask, returning to our interrogation. "What did she have to talk with you about?"

"Why should I tell you?" He's growing defiant. Maybe I should congratulate him on finding his backbone.

"If you answer my questions, I'll leave you alone and let you rot. If I ever get the chance, maybe I'll even lend my brain to this little project you've got going on with the military. I've thought about ways to kill every super on the planet, Dr. Krenzler...even you."

He ponders my words and favors me with half a smile. "Hrm...okay. Talked about my condition. She wants to...stop the experiments."

"And you, naturally, want to keep them going. How are they killing you, Doctor? Your body used to be a perfect engine of survival."

He moves his manacles, apparently trying to point at something. "See...for yourself."

Following his suggestion, I tap my glasses and take a look at him in a different light. His physical body is a radiation stew thanks to the accident that turned him into Titan. I have to zoom in to a molecular level to see what he's actually talking about. Then I see a familiar signature.

It's quantum radiation. They're using a variation of Captain Tomorrow's time travel technology to age his Titan cells to the point of death. Even with his body fighting back and constantly regenerating, it's not replenishing the lost cells fast enough. They weaken and die right before my eyes. As they do so, they give off a small level of gamma radiation—the same type of radiation seen in atomic decay and left behind on Captain Tomorrow's corpse.

I take the glasses off, unable to look at the losing battle anymore. "What else did you and Eva talk about, Doctor?"

"Hrm...she told me about Captain Tomorrow."

"Given your current state, you seem to be a newfound expert on the subject. I assume he helped develop your 'treatment?'"

He nods.

"Still," I say, "any theoretical discussions on quantum radiation fail to answer the more pressing question."

One eye on Krenzler's face opens a little wider. "What...question?"

I smile slightly as I feel my confidence starting to return. "Curious now, are we? You and I aren't so different after all. We both love a good puzzle."

He coughs but gives no other response. The soldier on the floor is breathing more rapidly now. I don't have much longer.

"The big question is, where is Captain Tomorrow now? I know the corpse is from the future, but that still leaves us with the man missing in the present. I know he's out there somewhere, but where is he hiding and why?"

"Why does he need to be anywhere?"

"What do you mean?"

"You have...hkk...a bad hypothesis. Making an assumption with no clear reason to believe it's true."

"What are you talking about, Doctor?"

"Point of origin. You and I...exist in the present. Captain Tomorrow...travels time. Why would he be on the same scale as us?"

"I never had any reason to assume otherwise."

"You don't know his origins...don't know where he came from or why he did what he did. Not knowing that, you can't afford to assume anything."

He makes a valid point. What does the word "now" mean to a man who exists outside the flow of time? A person who knows he's going to get stabbed in a certain building wouldn't hide in that building—he'd leave the area entirely. In Captain Tomorrow's case, the building is the present. For all I know, he's watching me from the Mesozoic Era, waiting for me to die. If I go first, history changes and he knows the coast is clear.

"You have no idea how much you just helped me, Dr. Krenzler," I say. "Your body might be dying, but your brain still has a lot to give."

"Only until...I can finally end it all."

I put my glasses back on and head to the ambulance door. "Just when I remember why I used to idolize you, you go and ruin it."

"Don't...care about your approval."

"You should. I possess the vision you lack. You wasted your life looking for a cure. If I was in your place, I would have harnessed that monster in you and turned it into something great. Your brain, that body. Imagine what you could have accomplished."

"You...would have been an even bigger monster."

"No. I would have been a god. Your curse is my miracle, doctor."

I jump out of the ambulance and march through the field of soldiers. By the time the alert has been raised, I'm back in my civilian clothes and waiting for Eva.

"That was a waste," Eva says when she finds me again. "Krenzler's on his way back to the prison and nobody's allowed to talk to him until he's received medical care."

"They didn't let you speak with him?" I ask innocently.

"Not after you got done in the ambulance," she says accusingly.

I try to play dumb—a game I never win. "Me?"

"An 'unauthorized person on the scene.' In other words, you."

"But they didn't identify me, did they?"

"No, but I don't appreciate being used as a diversion. I expected better from you, Rosey."

The words sting enough that I almost lose my trail of thought. I recover just enough to stand on tiptoes and brush aside a lock of hair near Eva's left ear. "Nice earring. You're missing one on the other side."

She pushes my hand away. "I must have lost it during the battle."

"I won't lie to you if you don't lie to me, okay?"

She gives an exasperated sigh. "Rosey, that's not how it works. I'm your lawyer. You tell me the truth or you go back to jail. Until you stop acting like the rules don't apply to you because you've got a big brain, I get to keep my secrets."

We walk on in silence, and she starts to outpace me. I'm used to having people get angry at me, but I'm not used to caring about it. What's more infuriating is that I don't understand why she's angry at me. Yes, I broke some laws, but none that weren't worth breaking. She should sympathize with that.

"In my defense," I say, "I had a valid reason. I needed Dr. Krenzler to give my thought process a jumpstart."

"And did he?"

I imagine a Rubik's cube without colors on it. Still only one way to put it together correctly, but without clues to tell me how to do it. I can either guess blindly or invent my own rules. And I know which I'm going to choose.

"Oh yes." I grin and stop just short of laughing out loud. "I have a lot of new evidence to consider."

#14: WHYS AND WHEREFORES

I'm driving down the highway with a man who once tried to vaporize the Washington Monument, and yet I feel like he's the one who's afraid of me.

"Let's say you have to go in front of a grand jury and list all the crimes you've committed in the past twenty-four hours," I say. "So far, you've assaulted a member of the United States military, impersonated an officer, and made illegal contact with an omega-threat superhuman. What else have you done that I might need to prepare a defense for?"

Rosey has no leverage for a change. His teleporter is broken, and without his toys he's just a guy. I could drop him on the side of the highway and leave him stranded, stuck with no lab to work in and no whiteboard to brainstorm on.

"I think it depends on what you classify as a crime," he replies. He pauses slightly between each word, which tells me he's thinking of some way to spin what he's about say. "I might have stepped out of bounds a little bit, but all my actions had a purpose. And, in the end, they got the okay from Miss Destiny."

"You mentioned that," I say. "But I bet she didn't actually say they were okay."

"Her actions demonstrated they were," he argues defensively. "She used a teleportation spell to get me out of the old lab I raided—"

"What?"

"—then when I reappeared in my apartment I found the teleporter I had taken was still with me—"

"What?"

"—but she had removed the stun gun I intended to use against Invisible Lad—"

Tires screech as I swerve wildly toward the side of the road. Once we stop, I barely manage to keep myself from grabbing Rosey by the shoulders and shaking him.

"What?!"

"Calm down. There's a reasonable explanation." Confronted by my outburst, Rosey inexplicably switches gears and refuses to back down. It's like he wanted a fight. "I had a prototype of my battle suit stashed away and had to see if it could function as the murder weapon. Invisible Lad followed me and I panicked. I hit him with some electricity but didn't torture him—I'm a good guy now, remember? Miss Destiny could have thrown me right back in jail when she arrived, but she decided to work with me—just like she decided to work with you by giving you those earrings."

My hand brushes by my ear, where one of my ruby studs is missing. "How did…who's to say the earring came from her? Or that it has any relevance to anything?"

"Dr. Krenzler noticed what you did in his cell. You might be able to pull one over on me now and again, but don't make a habit of thinking I'm blind."

Inwardly, I panic a little bit. I calm down when I remind myself that the earring would have disintegrated entirely upon going off, leaving no trace for anybody to find.

"As for how I know Miss Destiny gave them to you," Rosey continues, "if they were based on any sort of science they would have popped up on the sensors you had to go through to get to Dr. Krenzler's cell. But Miss Destiny's magic doesn't show up on any scanners, not even my own."

I turn on my blinker, accelerate, and start speeding back down the highway again. Doing so gives me some time to gather my thoughts.

"You don't know everything, Rosey," I snap a moment later.

"No," he admits, "but I'm pretty impressive when it comes to supers. How many other people with a mystical arsenal have you been hanging around with?"

"There's one nobody knows about. She's my ace in the hole."

"Oh really? Is it somebody I've met?" Rosey's face lights up. I've added a new variable to his equation.

"No." I keep my eyes focused on the highway. Masters City's skyline appears on the horizon, outlined by a deep red sunset. "Her name's Mei. She got arrested for larceny a few years back, and the case came across my desk because somebody witnessed her using powers during one of her crimes. I got the charges dropped because the witness didn't keep his story straight on the stand, but he was right about one thing: she's got some mystical abilities."

"You've had somebody who could potentially help counter Miss Destiny all this time and you haven't told me about her?"

"She's not a pawn, Rosey," I growl. "She's a teenage girl with serious issues. She was a firebug as a kid—fooled around with some hot ashes in her parents' fireplace and wound up burning the house down. Both parents died. That was when she was in grade school. Now she's in a depressed funk and relies on her powers to hide away from the rest of the world. She might help me here and there, but she's not somebody who needs to get drawn further into this life if we can avoid it."

"How does she hide away?"

"What?"

"You said she relies on her powers to hide away from the world," he explains. "What did you mean by that?"

I conjure up the image of Mei sulking at my table just before she let Miss Destiny take over again. My car's engine hums as I push the gas pedal down.

"The same way you hide in your formulas and equations," I lie. "It takes her out of the world for a little while, so to speak."

I finally risk a sideways glance at Rosey. His face has become drained of all emotion. Mentally, he's in the middle of an experiment, and I'm interfering with the results. The car hits a bump and sends a fresh ache through my body.

"Miss Destiny..." he mutters. I hope he's changing the subject. "I need to figure out why she's playing my games. She never did before." He shakes his head and blinks his eyes, remembering I'm in the car with him. "Anyway, you've explained the earrings but not why you used them to free Dr. Krenzler."

He clutches his backpack as he speaks. Part of me imagines him searching for a remote control to a hidden orbital weapons platform right now. But that wouldn't happen. Even if when angry, Rosey would never lash out at me...I think.

"I had already made the appointment," I explain. "He's my client, after all, and there was an incident a little while back where some soldiers went nuts and tried to cut him up. So I figured if I was there, I might as well ask him about the radiation you found on the bodies."

Rosey folds his hands in his lap like a teacher's pet. "I appreciate the help, as always."

"When I got there...well, let's just say I wasn't ready for what I saw." I take a long, slow blink, almost taking my eyes off the road in the process. "I knew they were experimenting on him, trying to kill Titan, but I didn't expect the process to do what it's done. I didn't think it through; I just wanted to give him a chance to escape the fate they had in store for him."

"Come on, Eva," Rosey admonishes me. "You could have wound up getting people killed doing that, and Titan always winds up back in jail anyway. You're not stupid, or I wouldn't associate with you. So what were you thinking?"

"You said we could use a distraction to lure out Captain Tomorrow," I counter. "I figured, what better distraction than one of the mightiest mortals on the face of the Earth? And maybe, just maybe, he'd get away this time. I sure as heck didn't think Paradigm was going to try to kill him."

His face darkens and he looks out the window away from me for a moment. "Yeah...about that. Dr. Krenzler getting released did help me realize something. I was...er, well...I was possibly—just possibly—off-base on my Captain Tomorrow theory."

"You mean you were wrong?" I ask.

"Wrong? No." His hasty reply speaks louder than his denial ever could. "The dead Captain Tomorrow is definitely from the future. But there's not necessarily a present-day equivalent, either."

"What do you mean by that?"

"As I said before, Captain Tomorrow views time differently. But I've been making a rudimentary error in my thinking. I've seen him as inhabiting the same times as we are, but in a different order. If we go from A to B to C, I was thinking of him as going from B to C to A. But he doesn't have to exist in all the same points as us. He could go from A to C without even touching B. In theory, at least."

"So this whole thing was a wild goose chase"

Rosey frowns and almost nods, but stops himself from doing so. "Maybe. Our present moves at a linear rate, like this car going down the highway right now. Captain Tomorrow's got more of an all-terrain vehicle. He can come and go as he pleases, so he just has to hop on our road when it suits him."

"So we don't know if he's here in our time or not." I chew my lip in frustration.

"Exactly. Since my conversation in the past with him, it's possible that he's actively avoiding this time period as a way of trying to escape his own death. Or maybe he's conducting his own investigation in the distant future. We don't have any way of knowing, unfortunately."

We continue in silence for a while, hearing only the sound of rubber on asphalt. Then, after I've considered the angles, I speak again. "Whatever. I still don't regret trying to earn Solomon some freedom."

"I never suggested you should," says Rosey.

"You saw him. You know what they're doing in that facility."

"They're killing him off, cell by cell. They're making progress on finally eliminating Titan, but it means a slow and painful death for Krenzler at the same time."

"Exactly. Kill him, imprison him, or release him. Don't torture him like that." I swallow and check my mirrors. "I gave him a fighting chance. It's better than watching Solomon sit in a room and wait to die."

"Given the level of care and security he's getting, I don't think the government is waiting for him to die, either."

"What do you mean?"

"They would have finished what Paradigm started if they just wanted Titan dead. The final shot could have been delivered by anyone with a gun. Titan had no more fight left in him."

"So you're saying they want Solomon to stay alive and suffer for his crimes?"

"Not exactly. The way I figure it, they're keeping him around until they can determine if the process will be a complete success. That means they're either trying to make a more controllable version of Titan or..." he trails off and mutters almost inaudibly, "something else."

"Care to elaborate?"

"It doesn't matter right now. All that matters is that neither of my potential options explain why Paradigm decided to nearly kill someone when he's always used nonlethal force in the past."

"Maybe we're dealing with more time travel...or mind control, or shapeshifting aliens."

"Nah." Rosey's eyes shine in excitement of something he hasn't yet figured out, but is close to discovering. "It's got to be something really juicy. At least, I hope it is. Sort of like how I hope that whatever you're hiding from me is worth it."

"What do you mean?" I touch my brow and find that I'm sweating just a little.

"Don't worry," Rosey says. "I'm not going to pry. I've got a more pressing matter to deal with."

"And what's that?"

Rosey's answer almost makes me lose control of the car.

"I need to team up with Paradigm."

#15: WE ARE NOT SO DIFFERENT

I'd much rather aim a giant laser at Washington DC than talk about conflict resolution. I know every cog and gear of the laser. I don't know the first thing about people.

It's about four in the morning and I haven't even thought about sleeping. Instead, I've gone over the upcoming conversation in my mind hundreds of times, replaying it from every different angle and trying to guess what might be going through Paradigm's head these days. Eva offered to join me, but I couldn't have her here. Every extra person is an extra variable, and the equation has already gotten too complex.

I head up to the same rooftop we spoke on the night I got out of jail and pull another device from my backpack. It's basically a rewired remote control, but with my modifications, it creates a high-pitched hum only Paradigm's super senses can detect. If he's in Masters City, he'll notice it, and quickly, just like a canine responding to a dog whistle.

I wait for a few minutes with no response, then hit the remote again. Or rather, I start to. A crimson blur speeds by me before my fingers can press down, snatching the device from my hand. The sheer speed at which he buzzes in knocks me over. Had I picked a slightly different spot on the roof, I might have gone tumbling over the edge. I wonder if he realizes that.

"Nice to see you, too," I say, picking myself up and wiping grit off my slacks.

Paradigm hovers above me, almost in the exact same position as when we spoke a few days ago. He glowers, as grim and unfriendly as ever. Then he tightens his fist, crushing my remote and letting its shattered remains fall to the ground.

"I should haul you back to jail right now," he says. His lips barely move, but his voice carries far.

"Technically, I was just performing a simple experiment with a home electronics device."

"You knew what you were doing. You try to know everything you can about me."

"Officially, we've barely even met. Most of our interactions were actually between you and my evil clone."

He tightens one fist, then the other, and says nothing. I can practically hear his blood pressure skyrocket. The response is intriguing. I apply more stimuli, pushing him a bit further.

"The legal system declared me wrongly imprisoned," I say. "You still believe in the system, don't you?"

"Of course I do," he hisses.

I pace a circle around the rooftop. He pivots in his levitating position, carefully watching me all the while. The flat concrete on the roof darkens beneath him, singed by the energy he burns.

"Are you sure about that?" I ask. "Based on what I observed between you and Titan, I have to wonder how seriously you take the whole, 'no killing, protect the innocent, every life is sacred' thing."

"I didn't kill Dr. Krenzler."

"No," I concede, "but you came close. Titan was already weakened by the government's attempts to 'cure' Krenzler, but you kept throwing your best punches."

"I didn't know about this cure. All I know is that you and your attorney were on the scene, probably instigating the whole thing."

I hold my hands up in mock disappointment. "That hurts. You know I've turned over a new leaf. Eva had just visited her client in prison. When things went bad, she called me in."

"And how did you get there so quickly?"

"With a teleporter. A currently broken one, unfortunately. I have a few gadgets here and there that the courts let me keep." I unsling the backpack from my shoulder and place it on the pavement. "You want to see what other tricks I've got tucked away here?"

He floats forward a few feet. The air around me gets hot. His eyes glow like burning coals.

"I'm trying to play nice here," I tell him. "You and I have the same goal. We both want to find out who killed Captain Tomorrow. But you have to fly around the world to stop tornados and rampaging monsters, while I can focus on one thing at a time. I'm an asset; don't be afraid to use me."

"Why do you care who killed Captain Tomorrow?" he finally asks. "For all I know, you did it and now you're trying to cover your tracks."

"Believe it or not, I liked Captain Tomorrow."

He breathes in and tenses even further. Interesting.

"No you didn't," he says. "You'd still be at large if he hadn't sabotaged your battle suit."

"What you don't know about me could fill the hard drive on an alien supercomputer, Paradigm. I liked Captain Tomorrow because, unlike you, he didn't take everything so darned seriously. He smiled—even made jokes once in a while. And he always treated our rivalry like it was a job, not like I kicked his dog."

"This isn't a matter of being on different football teams. You've tried to take over the world. I think that deserves more than a little hostility."

"Do you even know what I could have done with this world?!" I snap, unable to keep the frustration out of my voice. "Put me in charge and I would have solved the energy crisis, balanced the budget, and cured AIDS within half a year. I could have—"

I stop myself. This is not productive. And I'm through trying to save the world by conquering it—or so I keep telling myself.

"Whatever," I say. "I'm trying to extend an olive branch, and you're arguing semantics."

He drifts away from me, closer to the stars. "This is a waste of time. Who knows how many crimes I could have stopped instead of talking to you?"

"Not as many as you let yourself think. Your head isn't in the game. Maybe that's just because your most deadly nemesis has been released from prison, or maybe it's because one of your closest confidants has just been murdered. Or maybe it's because you know somebody with real power is planning to kill you."

He stops his slow rise into the heavens and tilts his head slightly. "What are you talking about?"

"You've been acting paranoid lately. Moreover, you're starting to look your age—well, maybe not your true age, but the years are finally taking their toll. You might have dominated that battle against Titan, but even in his weakened state he managed to land a few solid blows on you."

He opens his mouth, but just clicks his teeth together when he realizes that whether he confirms or denies my observations, he's giving me useful information.

"There's something else, too," I continue. "I think you know what's been going on in that prison where they're keeping Krenzler."

"They're working on a cure for him, just like always," he insists. "They're basing it on his own research, if I remember correctly."

"His own research," I confirm, "but with aid from somebody else. It's not just a cure, is it? It's a weapon, too."

He lowers his elevation a little, coming down closer to my level. "What do you know about Krenzler's work?"

"I know why General Lucas didn't just put a bullet in Dr. Krenzler's head when he had the chance."

His mouth twitches. "They were probably afraid of setting off another transformation."

"Given the beating you laid on him, even a transformation into Titan would have done nothing. The gray guy had nothing left. He's never been that weak and helpless before, which is pretty odd considering the number of times he's fought you and the rest of the supers in the area all at once."

His eyes widen. Now he's the one using me for information gathering—confirming the fears that have been lurking in the back of his skull.

"You see what I'm getting at," I continue. "You knew Krenzler's research was being used to weaken and eventually eliminate Titan. But you've got your code against killing—even if you wanted to, you know that just applying that little bit of extra muscle in one of your punches would bring you all sorts of scrutiny. Most people would probably give you a pass. After all, it's not like Titan is the easiest creature to control. But there would be a little doubt, a little piece of the population that would wonder whether having a nuclear man flying over them as a protector is really what they want, especially if that protector has crossed one of his best-known self-imposed rules."

He touches down and walks toward me until he's within arm's reach. "Are you saying I wanted the Army to kill Titan?"

I swallow and try to hide my nervousness as I continue, knowing what might well happen if I push him too far. "I can't say for sure, but I do think you wanted to see if they would do it when given the chance. But they need more than just a dead monster—they need to know how to kill him. They want to see each of his irradiated cells break down into nothingness. They're working to make sure they can take a fully powered Titan and eliminate him for good. And that's a possibility that should scare you."

He puffs his chest out, every bit the male ideal of fitness and strength. "Why should anything frighten me?"

"The same accident that created Titan created you," I answer. "You each run from the same energy source. He's your dark twin. What the government can use against him, they could use against you."

"The governments of this world never need to fear me."

"Once upon a time, that might have been true. But now we live in an era of terrorism and paranoia and fear. It used to be there were plenty of mad scientists and obvious bad guys to go gunning for. But you did your job too well; you caught all the villains. I spent five years in jail, and when the people of this world didn't have to worry about me pulling the moon out of orbit, they finally looked up and saw you.

"Fear is a drug," I continue, "and our society is addicted to it. And when the bad guys outside have all gone away, the people turn on themselves. They peer under their beds and glance in their closets. Or they look up into the sky and see you up there, invincible, ageless, and all-seeing. And then..." I work hard to keep from chuckling. It's not funny, but the irony is almost too much not to appreciate. "And then they started to think like me."

The air around us grows even hotter, but he's the one who starts to sweat.

"We live in a society that doesn't trust our superman anymore," I say in a low tone. "It sucks, doesn't it? To have the world suddenly turn against you. All you want to do is help them, but they won't listen anymore. You try to ignore it, but it gets under your skin. And then it stops being about altruism and turns into a quest to open their eyes and show them all. Of course, they won't realize you're still doing it all for them. All they'll see is the day you finally crack."

His smoldering gaze finally wavers. He takes a step back from me. All these years I've used weapons and robots in an attempt to hurt him. I didn't realize I could destroy him with words.

"I know you better than you think," I continue. "My release seemed too easy, didn't it? Even with Eva's skills and the lucky circumstance of the other-me appearing at just the right time, there should have been more paperwork and more resistance to letting somebody with my record off scot free. Maybe somebody pulled some strings behind the scenes. After all, if I was innocent or reformed, no harm done. But if I was the same old crazy Dr. Pythagoras, I'd go gunning for you again and maybe show them a thing or two about what their little project is missing." I do let a laugh escape this time, but it's a sad chuckle. "Everybody called me a villain, but in reality I was just ahead of my time."

I've paralyzed him. Now's the time to strike.

"It must be the McCarthy era all over again," I say. "You almost lost your place as the greatest superhero when that senator tried to convince America they couldn't trust a man who wore a mask. But back then you could stand behind your convictions and show the people that even if the country changed, your principles didn't. You got to fight it out in the court of public opinion, and you always won those battles. But now they're doing it behind closed doors and in covert operations. And those innocent people you stand up for aren't just blind to it, they're unknowingly complicit.

"This world we live in is filled with people who have seen so many mass shootings and natural disasters played live on social media that they're terrified of what might happen next," I add. "They've written the powers that be a blank check to stop the next disaster at all cost. They want our leaders to prepare for the worst case scenario, and they don't want to know the details. So there's no appealing to better judgment, no standing on your record, no pointing your fingers at any one supervillain or figurehead who's destroying the way of life you tried to protect. It's you against the world, old buddy. There's only one person on this whole planet who knows what you feel like right now, and that's me."

He puts on his stone face again. A heavy hand comes down on my shoulder and squeezes slightly. To him, it's comparable to trying to pick up an ant without crushing it. The force is enough to make the joint pop and send a jolt of pain down my arm. "You have no idea what my real weaknesses are," he says.

It takes effort to keep my voice level under the strain caused by this touch. "I think I do. And I think you're more alone than you've ever been before. Where were your superhero buddies yesterday? Whenever Titan got loose, even without the League of Liberty intact, your allies always responded in full force. But this time they were all gone, letting you do their dirty work. Are your friends all on the government's side, or are they just afraid of you, too?"

His eyes dart back and forth. His lips curl backwards, showing his teeth. "My friends...no, they're not my friends. None of them are."

"Not even Captain Tomorrow?"

"Captain Tomorrow is dead. And I'm almost certain you killed him."

"Technically he's not dead yet." My nerves get tense enough that my whole body shakes slightly. "The body that's been found is from the future. And it's not me who will kill him…it's you."

He flicks his wrist, casually tossing me to the ground. The impact tears the fabric off the knees of my pants. He held back enough to keep me from skidding over the edge and falling to the pavement a hundred feet below. I've made him angry, but he has enough restraint left to play human tiddlywinks rather than get serious.

I stagger back to my feet. I can smell my own sweat now. "Dr. Krenzler's cells are radiating high amounts of quantum energy. That technology used as part of his 'cure' is speeding up the process of entropy, causing the themodynamic process that powers his transformations to break down. They're artificially aging Titan's cells to the point of premature decay. I spent years studying that technology, but I never mastered it. The only person who knows how to make the process work that effectively is your supposed friend. You're going to kill Captain Tomorrow, but he tried to kill you first."

His face changes as the last piece of the puzzle clicks into place in his mind. I get a sudden wave of nausea as I realize that he didn't know about Captain Tomorrow's involvement until just now. He sways unsteadily, as if part of his body wants to rocket off into space and the other part wants to crush my windpipe. He looks like he's about to rip himself in two, and I'm the only one here who can save him.

"Come on," I say, extending a hand. "The world's going crazy. Team up with me and let's make some sense of it all before it's too late."

He reaches out and almost takes my offer, but then pulls away and looks at me like I'm diseased. "Team up? With a criminal like you?"

"Who else can help you fight the future? We're trying to prevent the murder of a time-traveler who has potentially allied with the government to work with a 110-year old scientist who transforms into a ten-foot tall engine of destruction when he comes close to death, all so he can prepare against the possibility of a nuclear-powered man from going rogue and destroying the country. To say that stranger things than us joining forces have happened is an understatement."

He almost takes to the air again. But then a strange expression comes over his face. He takes my hand and shakes it. For a fleeting moment, everything seems to be going according to plan.

But just like that, everything changes for the worse. His body grows hot again. He squeezes my hand, and two of my fingers snap like twigs. He releases my hand when I shout in pain, but his lips curl upward in a sadistic smile.

"Whether you're right or not, you're too dangerous to keep on the loose," he says. "If everything in this world is really pushing me to become a murderer, I might as well start with you."

He forms a fist that can knock down a skyscraper and aims the punch at my head.

#16: NO REST FOR THE WEARY

Splotches of purple and slashes of red have turned my body into a haphazard roadmap of pain. I wonder if this is what Rosey used to look like when he took a beating from the League of Liberty.

I stagger home in need of a bath, a change of clothes, and some first aid after today's fiasco. My shredded clothing drops along the hallway floor as I strip piecemeal on the way to the tub.

My bathroom is smallish, but well-appointed enough to have a nice deep clawfoot tub and a heat lamp. I close the door and turn the lamp on, setting it to half an hour. Then I turn the faucet on to a temperature just short of boiling and climb in. My feet leave dusty gray prints on the white tile, but I really don't care right now. I need to let the heat melt my tension away while I forget about things for a while.

Unfortunately, my mind just won't let me be.

Due to Solomon's transformation, the military won't allow me access until he's fully secured and no longer deemed a threat. I'll look into a motion to allow me to define what they mean by "threat" in the morning. Even so, security will be even tighter now. Solomon will have even less human contact. And if anybody ever finds out what I did to let him out, I'll be locked away too. Based on the sheer number of times I've violated my professional ethics in the past few days, I'm basically the newest villainess of the legal world. Rosey would tell me not to worry about little things like that—it's all part of a grander plan, which makes everything okay. That doesn't comfort me.

Right now, Rosey's out on a rooftop somewhere making preparations for his confrontation with Paradigm. I should have had Miss Destiny tail him. The last thing I need on top of everything else is to have Rosey go off the deep end and declare war on the big guy. If that happens, I don't know what kind of story I can spin to keep him out of a jail cell. Then again, maybe it's time I stopped making up excuses and went back to doing what a lawyer is supposed to do: defending people with facts.

I could have gone with a different tactic in getting Rosey out of prison. A psychologist might have diagnosed him with a number of different disorders that needed treatment at a proper medical facility, be it his obsession with defeating Paradigm, his delusions of grandeur, or his occasional bouts of narcissistic personality disorder. You can't try to blackmail the government into putting your face on a million dollar bill and not have a little something wrong upstairs. But I don't know if Rosey would have accepted that implication.

There's also a societal stigma to consider. Once you've been declared insane, people always label you as crazy. If you're an ex-con, you can turn your life around…as long as you have certain privileges on your side.

I close my eyes and don't open them again until I hear myself snoring.

I don't know how long I dozed, but the heat lamp is off and the bath has gotten cold by the time I wake up. Down the hall I hear voices and music. It takes me a minute to place the sounds, and then I realize what they are. Somebody has turned on my TV.

I keep my ears open for a few more minutes until I'm sure the intruder is sitting on my couch instead of wandering around looking for something. When I don't hear footsteps, my heartbeat goes back to normal. I pull the drain on the tub and step out. Then I grab a towel, dry off in the dark, slip on a large burgundy bathrobe, and head to the living room.

The smell of cocoa tips me off as to the intruder's identity before I see her. Mei sits in the dark on my leather sofa, sipping a cup of hot chocolate and transfixed by cartoons. It's some old superhero program from back when it was okay for Paradigm to beat up Russians in remarkably over the top ways. I turn on the light, and Mei scrambles for the remote, clicking off the program as though she was embarrassed to be caught watching it.

"Hey," she says, turning her head to look at me without moving her body from the couch. "Sorry I let myself in. You left your door unlocked."

"Hm." I grunt. I must have been even more exhausted than I thought. "How'd your date go?"

Mei flushes a little bit and fidgets. "Not bad, I guess. But I had to bail on him early."

"Why?"

"Oh, you know..." She makes a mock flex of her muscles. "Superhero stuff."

"Because of Titan?"

"No...because of your guy. There was this whole confrontation in the sewers, and...well, I don't know what happened exactly."

Right. Rosey told me about his meeting with Miss Destiny. For some reason, it never clicks that she and Mei can't be in two different places at the same time.

"The bottom line is she confiscated a battle suit that can supposedly beat Paradigm if it gets some repairs," she continues. "She and a couple other supers have been making sure it gets fixed up. She's been so focused on that, she never even noticed I swiped the earrings for you."

The earrings. I touch a hand to my left ear and notice I'm still wearing one of them. Pulling it off, I hand it back to Mei. "Unfortunately, there's only one left." Then I pause and glance at the TV, where the cartoon Paradigm was smiling and quipping—a stark contrast to the man I saw a few hours ago. "Wait a minute...why is she fixing it up? If it's a threat, shouldn't it be destroyed?"

Mei puts a finger on her chin, as though the thought hadn't occurred to her. "I dunno...come to think of it, one of the other supers said something along those lines—Invisible Guy, I think."

"That's Invisible Man," comes a voice out of nowhere.

I shout and jump to my feet, but the intruder moves faster. A fist comes out of nowhere and connects with my stomach. I double over and drop to the ground while Mei screams. The attacker knocks her glass out of her hand, and it breaks on the hardwood floor. When I push myself back to my feet, a man in an orange and white bodysuit has Mei trapped in a headlock.

"I knew if I followed you long enough, this would all start to make sense," he barks. "You agreed to play babysitter to Pythagoras, let him fry me without any consequences. I figured you were playing along with the lawyer, but I didn't realize you were just a kid playing at adult games."

"I'm not just a kid," says Mei through gritted teeth. "And Miss Destiny and I aren't the same person."

"Stow it. The grown-ups are talking."

I brush some stray hair from my face. "You're pretty condescending for a guy who started his career as a sidekick."

"I never thought I could scam the superhero community," he retorts. "Back when I was green, I knew my place."

"You don't know your place at all," Mei hisses angrily. "You're all too afraid of each other. That's why you're stalking Miss Destiny instead of going after actual bad guys."

Invisible Man places two fingers at the base of Mei's neck. "Keep running your mouth, kid, and I'm gonna put you down with a nerve pinch that will leave your head feeling like it got hit by a bullet train. You got anything to say about that?"

Mei looks at me and shrugs with her eyebrows. Then she says, barely audibly, "Mhasaz."

The thunderclap and resulting burst of purple smoke catches Invisible Man off guard. That his hostage goes from a small but portly teenager to a tall, statuesque adult in the blink of an eye doesn't help him either. Before the smoke can clear, I hear Miss Destiny shout another set of mystic syllables. A crackle of electricity flashes through the living room, and I hear the sound of a body hitting the floor. When the smoke clears, Miss Destiny is smoothing out her cape and Invisible Man lies unconscious.

I nudge the body with my toe. He groans, but remains motionless. "What did Mei mean when she said you're all afraid of each other?"

Miss Destiny runs a hand through her hair. "Surely, Miss Corson, you have noticed a lack of superhuman activity lately. There are fewer clients for you to defend and fewer of my allies on patrol. Even Invisible Man here has kept a lower profile than usual, except for the favor I asked of him earlier. My people are trying to figure out whom we can trust."

"Whom you can—" Then it hits me: the reason Paradigm had to go up against Titan alone instead of having allies at his side. "Rosey's on the right track. You're all afraid of Paradigm."

Miss Destiny's emotionless face flickers for a moment. The corners of her mouth turn downward, and her eyes grow sad. "There are…evolving beliefs in justice in our community. After Dr. Pythagoras broke up the League of Liberty, our members went in new directions. Some of them started to make preparations in case certain members were ever mind-controlled again. And others…just became paranoid."

"Paradigm doesn't trust you anymore, does he? And if he can't trust you, why should any of the other capes out there?"

"It is more than one man, Miss Corson. But yes, the fact that I have chosen to lend my aid to Dr. Pythagoras' rehabilitation has left my peers suspecting the worst."

"So who are they more afraid of? My client, Paradigm, or you?"

"Everyone," she says simply. She bends down and picks up the earring Mei had dropped when she transformed. "We can trust nobody."

I don't bother to offer any excuses. After all, I have none to give. My whole endeavor with Solomon wound up causing more harm than good. All it did in the end was prove to Rosey that he needed to confront…

"Oh God," I mutter. "If you're worried about Paradigm snapping, we need to find him right now. Rosey was planning to—"

I don't get a chance to finish my sentence. A high-pitched humming drowns out my voice. An explosion from downtown Masters City follows, accompanied by the sound of shattered glass.

#17: WRATH OF THE SUPERMAN

Why do I never plan properly for getting punched in the face?

It looks like somebody carved a manic grin on Paradigm's face. After decades living in a world of cardboard, he finally gets to let loose. Even if there's anything left of my body, no one will question his claims of self-defense. One word about crazy Doctor Pythagoras, and he'll be in the clear. Only those already working on his destruction in an underground lab will doubt him, and they'll probably be too worried that they're his next targets to do anything about it.

I touch a small plastic disk in my pocket before he unleashes the punch that spells my certain doom. The device makes a soft click as it triggers the fourteen speakers I planted in the area before I called him. It begins as a low hum, causing his eyes to water. He hesitates as a wave of nausea washes over him. Then the hypersonic transmitters hit their stride, creating an ear-piercing tone that causes him to let go of me and grab his head in pain.

The trap won't buy me the time I need. I planned against him trying to arrest me, not kill me.

I break into a full sprint the nanosecond he lets me free. Even when his eardrums start to bleed, I only pause long enough to throw the trigger disk off the building, ensuring Paradigm can't stop the sonic barrage. While his enhanced senses aren't quite what the media claims, they're still far above normal. The high-pitched squealing causes glass to shatter for blocks around. My eyes have swollen and my equilibrium is off. To him, it must feel like a steam train running through his inner ear.

"Stupid, stupid, stupid," I mutter as I throw open the roof access door and take the stairs two at a time.

I remind myself I'm wasting my breath by speaking, and promise to berate myself for my oversights later. Right now, my mind and body both need to be on the same page if I'm going to get out of here alive.

I jump from halfway down one fight to the landing, stumble a bit, and keep going. Running down ten flights of stairs is guaranteed to leave me out of breath by the time I reach the bottom, but taking the elevator means I'm stuck in a metal box once Paradigm recovers.

The distant rumble behind the fire alarms and breaking glass tells me he's identified the location of the speakers. He gives a shout as he smashes them one by one. By the time I reach the fifth floor, the sonic squeal has died out. At least it's easier for me to move and breathe now. Small blessings.

Paradigm soon reminds me of exactly how small that blessing really is. Plaster falls from the ceiling. A single punch collapses the rooftop. The building's steel girders buckle under the stress of his blow. Then the skyscraper collapses in on itself from the top down.

I throw open the door on the second floor and run straight across the hall toward a window. No time to look for a fire escape. I shield my face with my arms and hurl myself through the glass, barely dodging a falling beam as I make it out in the nick of time.

Dropping twenty feet into the middle of a crowded street is a less than ideal situation, but I've learned to take a fall. A car swerves as I plunge into its path. I tuck and roll, then I'm back on my feet and moving in a half-run, half-limp across the road. Traffic hits a standstill as the cloud of debris begins to settle and everybody stops to look at the human atom bomb up in the sky. I risk one glance over my shoulder. His eyes glow and his body burns hot enough to melt steel. I observed earlier that he hadn't been running as hot as he used to. I didn't realize at the time that it was predictive of a meltdown.

The sonics were Plan B. Getting out of the building brought me to Plan C. I've got backup plans that run the Roman, Greek, and Arabic alphabets. Unfortunately, Paradigm can punch through my contingencies as quickly as I can enact them. So let's just go straight to Plan Zay: running like hell.

The dust cloud and rubble combined with the car alarms and screaming gives me some obscurity from his eyes and ears. Unfortunately, he's also got a nose like a bloodhound. So I rush for the nearest sewer entrance and dig my electromagnetic gloves out of my backpack. They're useless in battle against Paradigm, but they allow me to lift and remove a manhole cover with barely any effort. Nothing like compounding my problems by having to run from a power-mad nuclear man *and* a feral group of intelligent bipedal carnivorous lizards at the same time. But hey—I love a challenge.

I get a good twenty seconds before the sound of clawed feet splashing through the tunnels greets me. I scramble up a ladder and nearly slip on the top rung.

Damn, damn, damn. I can't afford slow down, even for half a second.

Pushing the manhole cover open takes more effort than I suspected. When it finally opens, it does so with a nice loud metallic clang. But that doesn't matter. The lizards aren't going to reveal their presence to the surface world. As for Paradigm, he must still want to maintain his image as the protector of Masters City. The building he can blame on me, but he's not going to tear apart the streets looking for me, is he?

The sound of crumbling asphalt answers my question. He's not using reason—wherever he was mentally, it only took a single nudge to send him over the edge. I glance back to see a deep fissure opening up along Finger Street. Cars slide into the hole, some with passengers still in them. A water main bursts, and the spray turns into a cloud of steam as it evaporates against Paradigm's rage.

Then I witness something I once longed to see. The people of the city take one look at their former savior and run away.

Inadvertently, I've just accomplished what I always hoped to do—I've opened everybody's eyes. Unfortunately, I did it at the worst possible time.

Panicking as the fissure widens, people up ahead abandon their cars. I jump into the driver's seat of the one that has the clearest shot at open road. The owner didn't even bother to turn off the engine. Behind me, I hear a metallic popping sound, like a giant toaster just went off. I glance in the rearview mirror and slam my foot on the gas.

He's not flying after me anymore. He's on the ground, running through traffic. *Running through cars.* When his red-hot body doesn't just slice one in half, he tosses it to the side like a toy, smashing it to bits on the office buildings around us.

It's about letting off steam now. All that rage has boiled over, and he's just as angry at the rest of the world as he is at me. Unfortunately, he hasn't forgotten the man who set him off just yet. I need something bigger—something to really shake up his super senses and give me a chance to make my getaway.

A map of the city forms in my mind as I speed through the streets. I swerve through an obstacle course of abandoned cars and emergency vehicles. Due to the obstructions in my way, I can't hit a consistent speed above 40 miles per hour. Paradigm isn't hindered by such things, and he's gaining on me, his legs a blur as they move. I only have one chance—if I can't shake him now, I'm as good as dead.

I see a gas station up ahead and put the pedal to the floor. Paradigm streaks after me, his red uniform outlined by the blue and yellow sirens in the street. As the car closes in on the pumps ahead, I throw the door open and roll out. The fast-speed tumble leaves me with some bumps and bruises, maybe even a couple broken bones, but I'll live.

The car's momentum carries it through to the pumps. While I hadn't been thinking directly about it, my unconscious managed to carry out another important part of this plan: finding a particularly cheap car with low safety standards. The collision with the fuel tanks starts a fire, and that fire quickly erupts into a series of explosions.

Paradigm pulls up short as the sudden flare leaves him temporarily blinded. The roaring of the flames and the smell of burning gasoline is enough to finally render me obscured to his super senses.

I pick my aching body off the street and run toward an alley. Hidden behind smoke and screams, I chance a look back to see if my gamble worked. Paradigm has taken to the air again, ignoring the fire and floating higher and higher to get a better vantage point. With his skin lit up orange-red by the crackling flames of the fuel, he looks more demonic than I ever imagined he could. I don't linger long enough to give him a chance to spot me again—I dash into the maze of alleys and side streets, eventually disappearing back into the sewers.

How many innocent people have died because of my schemes and machinations? I can never say for sure, but the casualties are almost nonexistent and the major injuries are fewer than one would expect. I always run the numbers in these little encounters, and the most important variable is the sympathy of the supers chasing me. No matter what happens, they always hold the lives of others as their top priority, and they'll always pop up just in time to save the person I shoved out a window or the innocents I just threatened with my instant inferno. At least, that's what I used to count on. After tonight, I think a change in tactics is in order.

I pause in one of the sewer tunnels and rest my hands on my knees, taking a few seconds to catch my breath when I feel a sudden rush of cool air against the back of my neck. I turn around in time to see a shimmering ripple in space and time, as though they air had become water and somebody just tossed a rock into the well of reality.

"Things have gone bad for you, haven't they?" The voice is familiar, as is the shifting sensation of his materialization.

"I've hit some minor inconveniences, yes," I answer.

The ripple fades away, revealing a man wearing a black cowl and an hourglass symbol on his chest. The same man whose death triggered all these events.

"Hello Roosevelt," Captain Tomorrow says. "I think we're long overdue for a talk."

#18: THE NEVER-ENDING BATTLE

*E*ven when you can travel miles in the blink of an eye, sometimes you're just too slow.

With a clap of Miss Destiny's hands and the shout of a few words, my apartment melts away and we find ourselves on a battlefield. Invisible Man, whose unofficial job now seems to be getting electrocuted into unconsciousness, stays behind.

Just as I'm starting to think that Miss Destiny could teach Rosey a thing or two about comfortable teleportation, the noise and fire of the world around me shatters my senses. I barely recognize the neighborhood we land in. Overturned cars litter the area, some hurled through second-story windows with their drivers still inside. Broken glass crunches under my feet, shining in the glow of emergency lights like multi-colored shards of ice. My eyes water from the haze of smoke, and a thin coat of perspiration shines on my skin from air that's as hot as a furnace. Police are on the scene, but they make no attempt to clear the area. They don't have to disperse the crowd—everybody's already running away.

The crimson-clad avenger whose very presence could once calm a riot soars above us, ignoring the cries for help as he scans through clouds of smoke with his super vision.

"He could not have done this," Miss Destiny says.

"It doesn't matter if he did or not," I reply. "People are calling for help and he doesn't care. If there's anything more frightening than a vengeful god, it's an indifferent one."

One police officer with a megaphone tries to appeal to Paradigm, but does it in a profoundly stupid way.

"Paradigm, this is the MCPD. Please stand down."

Miss Destiny's eyes meet mine. We both have the same expression of shock on our faces, like we're watching a toddler stick a paperclip into an electrical outlet.

"Stand down now or we will be forced to open fire," the officer repeats, his hands shaking.

Paradigm looks at the little uniformed man on the ground, then at the squad gathering around him. He tilts his head quizzically and waits to see how far this will go.

I would hold these guys' actions against them if I didn't realize it was a direct result of panic. At least half a dozen officers raise their pistols and fire. They actually shoot handguns at the man who has shrugged off tank shells without so much as a scratch.

The attack works as poorly as any rational mind could have foreseen. Paradigm's left hand darts out in front of him in movements faster than my eye can see. He catches each bullet that comes within arm's reach. Then with a flick of his wrist, he sends them back at his attackers, one by one. Each of them gives a howl in turn as a piece of shrapnel hits their hands, forcing them to drop the gun and clutch their arms in pain. The last bullet hits the megaphone itself, muting the police's ineffectual bluster.

That was with just his left hand. Who knows what he might be able to do with his right?

"You are all being deceived," Paradigm says, speaking in a booming voice that doesn't need a megaphone to enhance it. "None of you ever need to fear me, as long as you don't do anything stupid. The person who tricked you—who tricked all of us—is hiding, but I intend to find him and give him the justice he deserves. Nobody can stop me, and nobody can hide from me for very long." He flies higher, his glowing eyes seeming to look at everybody at once. "Rest assured, I have not forgotten any of you. And you will all be protected."

"How are we all protected when there are buildings on fire?" I ask in a hiss.

"He is not himself," Miss Destiny says. "I will handle this."

She waves her hands and a gust of wind sweeps through the streets, lifting her into the sky with her cloak billowing behind her like a dark blue cloud. As Paradigm gives Miss Destiny his attention, the police and paramedics rush to fix the collateral damage in front of them before more comes their way.

"Paradigm, you need to stop this," Miss Destiny says, her voice an octave higher than usual. "There are people in danger right now, and they need you to protect them."

Paradigm gives her a dismissive wave. "That would be treating the symptoms, not the disease. The chaos is all part of his plan. He's using it to slow me down while he makes his next move. I've wasted too much time playing a madman's games instead of just dealing with him when I had the chance."

Miss Destiny holds her arms parallel to the ground and puts her palms flat. White energy crackles around her, and then she drops her arms back to her side. "Dr. Pythagoras is not in the area," she says. "That means you are putting lives at risk by wasting time."

"I'm not talking about—" He stops and narrows his eyes. "Why would I trust you? You've been working with Pythagoras from the start."

"I have been monitoring him, not working with him."

"And your 'monitoring' got dozens of people killed. You're just as guilty as he is."

Paradigm clenches his fists, and that's all the reason Miss Destiny needs to lash out. She waves her hands, creating a shimmering set of manacles around Paradigm's wrists.

"Something is wrong with you," she says. "You need to leave immediately."

Paradigm says nothing…just stares at her with the ugly, stupid expression of somebody whose mind can't comprehend a nonviolent solution.

"Do not waste your time trying to break free," Miss Destiny says. "Just as magic has always been one of Pythagoras' blind spots, it has been your weakness as well."

The air around Paradigm ripples as he gives off more and more heat. Beads of sweat form on Miss Destiny's brow.

"I. Have. No. Weaknesses!" With a strain and a shout, Paradigm shatters the magical manacles. They crackle with electricity and then disappear. "None! Do you understand?"

Miss Destiny crosses her arms in front of her just in time to summon a glowing shield that absorbs a blow from Paradigm. Still, the force of the punch knocks her into a building across the street. She emerges from the inside of an empty office a second later, flying slowly and warily. But Paradigm's on her again in an instant, hammering away at her shield with his nuclear fists.

"No weaknesses!" he yells. "I've fought Pythagoras and Titan and everything else that has been thrown against me, and nobody has beaten me! I've protected this whole planet and never asked for anything in return! Now you dare to call me the problem?!"

It's not easy, but I manage to tear my eyes away from the battle. Rosey was here moments ago, and I have to find out what he's done. More importantly, I have to find out if he really caused all this.

Ignoring the crash of Paradigm's fists and Miss Destiny's mystical shouts, I try to retrace Rosey's steps. I know he was going to meet Paradigm on a rooftop. I wanted to be there with him, but he refused. He said he had a defense if things went bad. What could that be?

My eyes scan across the smoking skyline. The destruction seems to be more focused above street level—a bell tower, a satellite dish, a couple smashed office windows. You planted some sort of sonic trap in the area, didn't you Rosey? That must have bought you enough time to get out of the building. But did they have an unexpected effect? Did your sonics screw with Paradigm's brain somehow?

Miss Destiny gives a shriek of pain, which breaks me out of my thought process. Paradigm has shattered her shield and now has her in a bear hug. That would be enough to cripple her for life, but she reacts fast enough with another spell. A giant green fist materializes behind her and rips Paradigm away, tossing him into the sky like a pebble. The reprieve is only momentary, as he regains control over his flight and comes rocketing back at her.

I look away again and try to focus on what I can control. I'm a lawyer. I don't fight supers, I only defend them in court after the damage has been done. And right now the damage my client might have caused goes far beyond the billions in property destruction.

You had a hidden lab in the sewers, right Rosey? That would be the perfect place for you to hide. Thick pipes and all sorts of ambient noises to confuse Paradigm's senses. But then, you can't confuse Miss Destiny's spells, and your teleporter broke after the encounter with Titan. Why didn't she detect you? Was she lying, or do you have even more surprises that you didn't tell me about?

The battle in the sky drifts away from the ruined city block, and I take off running after it, trying to keep Miss Destiny in sight. I don't know all the details about the magical timeshare she and Mei have set up. If Miss Destiny dies, what happens to the girl I've been trying to protect?

I might find out. The rapid castings start to take a toll on her, while Paradigm seems tireless. The glowing fist takes clumsy swings at the crimson-clad avenger, but he's moving almost too fast to see. Miss Destiny throws up shield after shield, but Paradigm shatters each one as quickly as it comes into existence. Finally, the crazed superman decides he's had enough. He waits until the fist almost lands a blow, then uses his super speed to maneuver behind Miss Destiny before she has a chance to blink. He extends his forefinger, flicking her in the back of the skull. Of course, when you're talking about Paradigm, that finger might as well be a bullet.

The green fist and the rest of Miss Destiny's energy projections blur and disappear. I pick up my pace as she tumbles limply from the sky.

Unfortunately, I am nobody's hero. By the time I reach her, she's lying motionless on a cracked sidewalk.

Paradigm lands next to her. I throw myself at him in a blind tackle. He swats me with a casual backhand, not even looking in my direction. I feel the impact in my bones before my mind registers that I've landed ten feet away.

Paradigm puts his foot on Miss Destiny's chest. He presses down with the very tip of his toe, but that's enough to draw a cry of pain from her lips.

"Say it," he hisses.

Much to my surprise, Miss Destiny still lives—and still struggles against her assailant. "Paradigm…you are not well."

He presses his foot down a little bit more. "Say it!"

Lips trembling, blood pooling underneath her, she finally gives in. "Mhasaz."

There's the burst of purple smoke. By the time it clears, Paradigm is in the air again. Mei kneels, her head bowed, but thankfully without any of the severe injuries that Miss Destiny had.

"I don't kill," Paradigm says. "I never kill." He gestures behind him, pointing back toward the destruction he just left. "I will bring the person responsible for…that…to justice."

He rockets back into the sky, leaving a burning city and a terrified populace behind.

I pick myself up and walk gingerly to Mei. Kneeling down next to her, I wrap her up in a hug. Then we do the only thing we can do at this moment. We huddle together in fear.

#19: FALLEN HERO

A war without end rages on the streets above. I can't tell if Paradigm's getting closer or if he set off a chain reaction in the streets and collapsed the entire downtown area.

Down here, I finally stand face-to-face with the man whose fate is linked with mine. Captain Tomorrow and I are both living on borrowed time—and I might have set the clock.

"I'm a little busy right now, Cap," I say. "Maybe you could do me a favor and jump back to yesterday. While you're at it, could you please warn me against talking to Paradigm?"

He puts a hand on my shoulder without answering me. An electric blue crackle of energy surrounds us. Reality rearranges itself around us, and I recognize the familiar nausea of instantaneous teleportation.

We materialize far away from the noise and destruction, and I can only imagine that Paradigm's mood is going to get worse once he realizes I've made it beyond his reach. We stand in a room big enough to store a jet plane, lit by fluorescent lights that still leave the distant ceiling covered in spotty shadows.

I blink my eyes rapidly. "A secret lair. I figured you'd be well-prepared enough to have something like this."

The walls are gray stone, with a bit of dampness to them. The roughness of the carving suggests this was once a natural cavern.

My mind sketches a map of the city as I try to figure out where this place might be hidden.

We're close to an electrical grid, at least—Captain Tomorrow landed us in front of a computer that would take up the entirety of Eva's living room. The blinking panels and array of buttons in a variety of different languages suggest he has more programming skill than I expected. Maybe on his best day, he might even be able to keep up with me for a few minutes. The rest of the cavern is filled with secrets of the superhero trade—spare costumes, special weapons, even a few trophies from old cases.

I press the toe of my sneaker into the ground. Given the color and consistency, I'd say the cavern is primarily limestone. We're probably below a large building in an industrial area. Captain Tomorrow's suburban home wouldn't be an appropriate front...too close to the city's substructure. Maybe a warehouse just outside the city limits...?

"This is how it's going to work," Captain Tomorrow begins. "I'm going to talk, and you're going to listen."

"Sure, sure." I nod while keeping my mental notes. If he has this area in addition to the secret walls in his normal residence, that must mean this place has added strategic significance. Then it hits me: it's a true secret hideout...a place Paradigm doesn't know about, and one that was probably built years ago without his knowledge. "But you make it sound like I'm the one who did something wrong here," I continue. "When you get right down to it, you should be the one listening to me."

"How do I owe you anything, after all you did?" He seems more than a little irritated that my eyes keep focusing everywhere else in this lair except for on him.

"Given what I estimate to be your current age and what I've deduced from our time-displaced corpses, I'd say we each have a matter of weeks left to live. And none of this would have ever happened if you had acted like the hero you pretend to be. What do you really want, Cap?"

"The same thing I've always wanted: to protect people."

"Then why are you half-assing it?"

He tilts his head in such a way that I can almost see the puzzlement under his mask. "What do you mean?"

"You're the time traveler. I'm the genius. I've devised more Paradigm-killing technology than any other being in this universe. If you're going to buddy up with the government and try to figure out a way to kill my arch-nemesis, then I should have been the first call on your list. Heck, you could have jumped back in time and stopped yourself from damaging my battle suit five years ago. Then none of this would ever have happened."

He shakes his head. "It's not that easy. If Paradigm dies five years ago, nobody's here to stop the Bronze Brain when he brings an army from one of Jupiter's moons."

"I would have been."

"You can't do what Paradigm can do."

"Yes! I! Can!" My shouts echo off the walls. "Don't you get it? *I* am this world's protector! If I can't do something today, I'll invent a way to do it tomorrow! The only thing you and the other self-proclaimed heroes have ever accomplished is keeping me from putting humanity in a position to protect itself! I see possibilities you could never have dreamed. And now I'm mere weeks from death, all because your small mind couldn't accept the simple fact that you need *ME!*"

He takes a step back, then stares into his own open hands. "Dear God," he whispers in a barely audible voice, "is this really how far I have to go?"

"You have to excuse me," I say, as though my outburst didn't happen. "I just nearly got my head knocked off by the supposed protector of America. And I can't help but feel he wouldn't be this aggressive if he hadn't found out that his best friend has been plotting against him."

"I wasn't—" He sighs. "I was trying to put a failsafe in place. There are so many possible futures…I just wanted to prevent one of the bad ones."

He turns to his computer and punches some buttons. A series of flickering images show up on a dozen different monitors, each depicting some sort of apocalyptic wasteland. Shattered buildings.

A desert of glass. One shows the melted slag of what might once have been the Statue of Liberty, and another has only the burned out steel girders of a building next to a sign that faintly reads "RP Industries."

"I was born a hundred years from now," he says, "and this shattered future is all I ever come home to. I've spent the best years of my life darting back and forth in time trying to fix it, and I never get anywhere. It all started tonight."

"Are you saying Paradigm did all this?" I ask.

"No. I'm saying you did." He points at each screen in rapid succession. "Everything gets old and gives in to entropy—even a mind. Paradigm's starting to lose himself. He's getting paranoid."

"It's not paranoia if they're actually out to get you."

"If I had broken you out of prison, what would you have done? Built a bigger death ray or gone after him in your metal suit. You never back off from the causes you lock yourself into. For Heaven's sake, I tried to warn you away from your present course, and all it did was get you more deeply engrossed in this puzzle!"

"No," I correct, "what got me more into the puzzle was the fact that you, the guy who can tell the future, were so clueless about it. I'm sure you've explored the various futures out there and figured out who does the deed, yes?"

He turns his head, taking his eyes off me and looking toward a blank wall in the cave. I cackle in amusement.

"Ha!" I chortle. "You still haven't?! You literally have all the time in the world, and you can't use it to save yourself?"

"All the time in the world just means I have an infinite number of different possible ending points," he says grimly. "There's something out there creating a blind spot, cutting off my ability to see the futures I need to—I didn't even know the full details about this situation until you told me about it in the past. With that in mind, there are only a few possible places I can travel to without risking a temporal ambush. Do you have any idea what it's like to walk around blind, knowing there's a blade with your name on it but never knowing when it's going to strike?"

"I fought Paradigm, remember? I dealt with that every day, because I always knew it was only a matter of time before he snapped."

He sighs. "And it always comes back to Paradigm. For all your genius, Roosevelt, you have a small mind."

My face curls into a snarl. "You dare—?"

I thrust a finger against Dr. Tomorrow's chest. But then I let my arm drop to my side. He's right. And the worst part is, I know he's right. I could have overridden the security system in prison and disappeared without a trace. But what would I have done? Set up a base on the moon and gone back to my old tricks. Build a giant robot or hatch a plan to devolve Paradigm into his monkey-like ancestor. I needed the break so I could get over my obsession. But now here I am, fighting the same old battle again. Only this time, I'm underprepared.

"Okay," I say when I've sufficiently recovered. "I need to add new variables to my equations. What's your grand scheme?"

"I don't have schemes, Roosevelt. I have hopes. The best hope the world had was you leaving this case behind. It would have taken some pressure off of Paradigm—kept him from going over the edge until we had a better way of dealing with him. But I can only bend time; I can't break it. And I can't change human nature, so the hope that you would do what was right was always a slim one."

"You self-righteous ass," I hiss through gritted teeth. "You don't get to blame me for this one. If Paradigm has been as vulnerable as you say, he needed somebody to reel him in. I've got Eva keeping me in check; he could have had you. Instead, you hid in another time and hope that somebody else…" I take a short breath and blink. "…that somebody else would kill him."

Then it hits me—Captain Tomorrow is standing in front of me, and he's hoping that I'll kill his best friend. How long has he fought beside Paradigm, knowing it would lead to this? When the League of Liberty split up, was it an after-effect of my mind control, or was the schism always inevitable?

"So this is what for you?" I ask. "Plan C? Plan X? How far down your list of contingencies do you have to be before you turn to me?"

He grasps the edges of his cowl and pulls off his mask, revealing the face of a man that I last saw dead on a slab. I take a few steps back. Even though his secret identity became public the day he died, this is against the rules. There's always a mask between me and them.

"It's the last hope," he says. "I've seen a thousand futures, and he always manages to beat you. But with what I'm giving you now, this nightmare might end."

What he's giving me…a room full of time travel technology whose secrets even I never managed to crack. Screens that allow me to see into alternate dimensions. The ability to know what my opponent will do before he does it. It's the extra edge I've always needed. But it's also too good to be true.

"You're lying." I feel the blood rush to my face as I speak. "You're going to hide somewhere in time and hope nobody kills you while you set me up for a fall. Meanwhile, you're playing both ends. If Paradigm wins, he claims this was all some sort of mind control and goes right back to being a hero long enough for you to find a new way to put him down. If I win, I become history's greatest monster for killing the world's first superhero. No matter what happens, this ends badly for me. And you think I'm stupid enough to follow your candy trail."

He doesn't even blink. "Even if you're right, would it matter? Does knowing the future change it?"

Captain Tomorrow takes a step backwards and removes a small black cylinder from his belt. He presses a button and a familiar crackle of electricity surrounds him. "Goodbye, Roosevelt."

With a flash, he disappears, leaving me with the bitter taste of futile rage in my mouth.

Captain Tomorrow is manipulating me. Maybe he always has been. Stupid old Roosevelt Pythagoras—the super-genius who doesn't know how dumb he really is.

I'm an alcoholic locked in a brewery. Everything Eva and I have worked for relies on me following the law and rehabilitating myself. But now I have the secrets of time travel in front of me. I have a righteous cause that I've always known to be more important than myself. And I've got the knowledge that, no matter what I do, I'll always be a villain in the eyes of the people.

Whether I'm being manipulated or not, it doesn't take nine PhDs to know how many choices I have. Anybody can count to one.

I crack my knuckles as I approach the computer console. Then I get to work, exploring the secrets Captain Tomorrow left behind for me.

I whisper a short apology to Eva. And I fall.

#20: INVERSION

Just standing near a superhero battle nearly crippled me. I can't imagine what Miss Destiny, having been on the wrong end of a slugfest with Paradigm, feels like. Wherever she is, I don't think she'll trading places with Mei for a while.

It seems like days before the elevator doors open to my apartment's hallway. Neither of us spoke the entire trip home. Our brains are so numb that it takes me time to realize that someone left the door open and turned on the TV.

"You can't assume this is Paradigm's fault," a news pundit says. "You give the guy who single-handedly won World War II the benefit of the doubt."

The counterpoint chimes in. "And how many cities get destroyed while we're waiting for answers? This incident needs to be dealt with like a terrorist attack—we need fast, decisive action."

"And what sort of action are we going to take?" the first one barks. "Shooting a missile at Paradigm will just annoy him."

"Well, maybe it's time to talk to Roosevelt Pythagoras. Maybe it's time we all started thinking more like him."

"Oh please. For all we know, he's the one who really caused this."

Somebody inside my apartment turns the TV off. Judging from where the broadcast got cut off, I have a good guess at who invited himself in.

"Rosey, what are you doing here?" I ask.

He doesn't acknowledge us when we first walk through the open door. Bloodshot eyes stare intently at a blank television screen. His face is unshaven, and it looks like he hasn't slept in days.

"I hope you don't mind. I had to let myself in," he says, still watching the empty screen.

"What happened to the invisible guy?" Mei asks.

Rosey stands up and grins, finally shaken out of whatever world he was just in. He bows in Mei's direction. "You must be Mei. You know, I always hypothesized that Miss Destiny had a dual identity, but I never realized she actually shared time in this world with another person—and a minor, no less."

Mei shrinks back, leaning closer to me. "How…how did you figure that out?"

"He's Roosevelt Pythagoras," I say. "He figures everything out eventually."

"Not entirely true, my dear," Rosey retorts. "In fact, I still wouldn't suspect it if I hadn't witnessed the change myself."

"You were there during the battle?" Mei asks.

"Not at first," Rosey replies. "And, quite honestly, I had to be very careful with my timing. If I had appeared a moment before Paradigm became occupied with Miss Destiny, he would have caught me with his super-senses and caved my head in. It took me a little bit to get used to the jumps. I had to knock out Invisible Lad in four separate timelines before I finally figured out when he would leave your apartment before I arrived."

Mei looks at me and shrugs. I decide to state the obvious.

"Rosey, you're not making any sense."

"Eva, I've had the most amazing past few days."

"You mean between Titan and then Paradigm nearly destroying the world as we know it?"

"No, no, no. I'm talking about the days after that."

"Rosey, that was hours ago."

"To-may-to, to-mah-to."

"No, not to-may-to, to-mah-to!" I yell. "That's a pretty big difference. What's happened to you?"

"Apologies," he says. "It's not often that I discover the secrets behind time travel, and I'm only just beginning to touch upon the possibilities."

"Time travel? Then you found Captain Tomorrow?"

Rosey grins like a jack-o-lantern. "Oh yes." He then drops the conversation and heads toward the kitchen. "Make yourself at home. Can I get you anything to eat?"

"It's *my* home!" I yell after him. Then, as an afterthought, "and I need some Scotch."

Mei and I drop onto the couch and nearly fall asleep despite ourselves. Then, in what seems like less than a second, Rosey's back with a double of Scotch for me and some cocoa for Mei.

"I'm sorry I didn't stop Paradigm's assault on Miss Destiny," he says to Mei. "Not that I could have just yet. Even when I put the finishing touches on my newest plan, I can't go back and stop that from happening. Causality-wise, it's not the right time."

I thought I had seen Rosey happy before. He was thrilled when he got out of jail and downright ecstatic when I gave him a chance to investigate a murder that hadn't technically happened yet. It turns out those were just a kid eating a piece of candy. This—whatever this is—is a kid who just found the keys to an entire candy store.

"Rosey, I need you to calm down and explain what's going on…preferably in as few words as possible."

"Mei can tell you part of it," he says, "provided that she knows some of what Miss Destiny does."

I glance at Mei. She looks confused for a moment, and then a look of realization slowly starts to dawn on her.

"Captain Tomorrow gave you his technology," she says.

"Exactly," he says. "Several supers wanted a contingency plan against Paradigm, and most of those plans involved me in some way. That much should have been obvious when Miss Destiny caught me underground and let me go in exchange for my battle suit prototype. I assume she's already brought it to some people who can fix it up and get it ready for the impending life and death struggle."

"Rosey, that's ridiculous" I say.

"Maybe not," Mei replies faintly. "I don't remember all the details when she's in control, but I know we went to a strange warehouse recently, and she's been in touch with a few of the techs that used to work on the League of Liberty's robots."

"Tell her she's wasting her time," Rosey says, waving his hands as though he were performing dozens of different mental calculations while speaking. "The battle suit was barking up the wrong tree. I have a new weapon that will be much more effective."

"Wait, what?" I stand up, shifting the focus of attention from Rosey to myself. "New weapon?! Rosey, we're not doing that. You can't do that right now."

Rosey raises an eyebrow, looking genuinely puzzled at my statement. "Why not?"

"Because your whole life is in shambles! People are in a panic over Paradigm going ballistic, and once they find out you were at the scene when he snapped, they're going to assume you're the guy who did it. You can't step into the supering business right now—not even if you think you're on the side of the good guys."

"Eva, you're thinking like a lawyer," he says in a dismissive tone that makes me grind my teeth. "And that's great—I mean, your legal abilities are the reason why I'm in this fantastic position right now. But the time for legal wrangling is past. I'm not worried about public opinion. By this time next week, the legal system won't even apply to me. You see, once I make my proclamation at City Hall—"

"No! No, Rosey, no! Don't go off the deep end right now! I don't need to be hearing about half-baked plans for world domination—especially not when the guy who's always beaten you before is out for blood!"

Rosey falls silent for a moment, and I can see a light behind his eyes as his brain processes some new information. I glance at Mei. She looks like she's going to be sick.

"Okay," Rosey finally says. "I get it now. I've been spending so much time jumping around that it's impeded my ability to communicate linearly. My point is that it's too late for me to worry about my legal standing. Think of Paradigm as a nuclear reactor that's gone into meltdown. We can't waste time dealing with an investigation to find out who's responsible. We have to act now before this disaster kicks off a chain reaction. By my calculations, we have a matter of days—your time, not mine—to stop Paradigm. If you're worried about salvaging reputations after that, I suggest you hold a press conference and deny any association with my actions. Sever ties with me completely and you can probably avoid getting listed as an accessory after the dust has settled."

"I'm not going to do that," I insist.

A strange spark lights up behind Rosey's eyes as he responds. "Maybe you should hear about my new plan before you make that decision."

"What plan?"

"A team," he says with manic glee. "It's what Paradigm had and I didn't all those times before. Even after the League of Liberty dissolved, he had allies he could call on. Sometimes, they made the difference between defeat and victory."

"But he doesn't have a team anymore," Mei protests. "I mean, not even Miss Destiny—"

"I'm never going to underestimate Paradigm again," Rosey snaps. "Even if it seems like he's alienated everyone, he'll still surprise me. To save the world, I need help of my own."

I storm right up to Rosey, emphasizing the height difference between us. "You are not talking about what I think you're talking about. I did *not* help you get out of jail just so you could put together some evil league of evil. If you even think about taking that step, I will knock you out and drag you back to jail myself!"

For a split second, Rosey starts to shrink away. But that moment vanishes in the blink of an eye. He keeps his composure, staring at me evenly despite my attempt to be physically intimidating. He just took on a guy who can crush coal into diamonds; there's only so much I can do.

"No supers on this team," he says coolly. "If there's one thing that the past few days have shown us all, it's how unreliable they can become." He glances at Mei. "No offense intended."

"So what else is there?" I ask. "Unless you play ball with the military, there's not a lot of options when it comes to actually trying to hurt Paradigm."

"I don't need brawn, Eva. I need brains."

"Who can with you in that department?"

He grins and touches a device on his belt that looks like an old Walkman. "Just watch."

My apartment vanishes in a flash of light. Mei, Rosey, and I reappear in an underground lair that puts Rosey's old volcano lab to shame. Then, once I get over the dizziness of the teleportation, my head really starts spinning.

Several dozen Roosevelt Pythagorases populate the massive cave, each working on some device or another. Some look younger with a full head of hair, others look older with wrinkles and sagging skin. One grizzled version has a scar over his left eye and a hook for a hand. Another looks like he's only about twelve years old.

The other Roseys pause in their job and wave in my direction.

I glance at Mei. Her jaw, like mine, is practically on the floor.

"Meet my team, ladies," Rosey announces triumphantly. "Are you ready to hear the rest of my plan?"

#21: I AM LEGION

*T*he memory didn't exist until I put it there. A little boy with a bloody nose, sitting alone on the playground. Abandoned by the other children because he doesn't belong, looked down upon by his teenage classmates because he's still a kid. He doesn't cry; he just touches the blood on his face, analyzing the sensation.

Don't get sad, kid. Get angry.

"Entropy ray, huh?" The voice sounds familiar but strange all at once. The boy turns to see a balding man leaning against the chain-link fence.

"It could work," the kid says with a sniff. "I just haven't figured out exactly how yet."

"Oh, I know Roosevelt. I know."

"How did you know my name?"

"How do you think?"

He frowns and furrows his brow. I was never cute as a child—I always looked like a scowling professor, even before I hit puberty.

"You know me by name and we seem to have something beyond a passing resemblance, so I'd guess you're a version of me from the future." He speaks matter-of-factly, devoid of the wonder a child should have when faced with the impossible. "Which I suppose invalidates the theory that meeting yourself while time traveling will cause a major disturbance in the fabric of space-time."

"If you're right, would that bother you?" I ask.

"No." He sniffs and wipes the rest of the blood off on his sleeve. "It means I'm a master scientist at some point in the future. And it probably means you need me for something important."

"Oh, I absolutely do, kiddo."

"You should realize we don't like being talked down to," he says with a bit of genuine hurt in his voice.

"Sorry," I say sincerely. "I'm just trying to figure out a naming system than can let me keep all the alternates straight."

"All the alternates?"

I step forward and offer myself my hand. "I need a team of the smartest people in the world. Call it narcissistic, but that happens to be me in just about every year of my life."

My younger self takes the hand, and we disappear into his future.

Previously, I had never met any alternate version of myself. Now I've done it a dozen times over. Future versions, beings of nothing but possibility who might become forever altered or entirely erased because of this experiment, now have these memories as well. There's no past and there's no future anymore. There's just the now, existing in every era and every possible reality. There's me and me and me, and the single unending passion that drives every iteration of Roosevelt Pythagoras, no matter what age and no matter what timeline.

In the present, or the past, or the future—it's really all the same these days—Eva and Mei look at the scene with a mix of horror and confusion on their faces.

"Rosey, what have you done?" Eva asks.

"After I escaped from Paradigm, Captain Tomorrow appeared and informed me of the situation," I explain. "Our government's been researching ways to destroy Paradigm if he ever goes rogue—the same crimes they would have let me rot in prison for."

Mei pipes up. "Yeah, but...well, the government hasn't created a death blimp or anything."

"Obviously, our appointed leaders lack imagination," I retort.

A smile crosses Mei's face, but disappears in an instant as she realizes I'm not joking.

"Based on the evidence I've gathered," I continue, "Paradigm's gone down an irreversible path. He's tasted blood now, and he won't stop until all the threats he sees have been eliminated. The only way to keep him from turning against this world and its people is to take him down. Other people—people who used to be against me—have finally seen the light. With a little assist from Captain Tomorrow, I can do this. And," I sweep an arm toward the lair full of time-displaced Roosevelt Pythagorases, "I've done a bit of recruiting to help me out."

"Rosey," Eva says, her voice filled with an unfamiliar chill, "you're insane."

My pulse rises at that statement. I breathe in sharply, but manage to keep my cool. "No, Eva. I'm proactive. That I'm dealing with technology others don't understand makes me seem mad, but I know what I'm doing. Roosevelt 51!"

"Yo!" comes a shout from across the cavern.

"Come on up and tell us about where you come from!"

"Roosevelt 51?" Mei asks. "How many of you are there?"

"Oh, not 51, I assure you," I state. "We decided to refer to ourselves based on our age. My original idea involved me being Roosevelt Prime and everyone else being Roosevelt 1, Roosevelt 2, and so on, but there were some...objections."

A Roosevelt Pythagoras who is almost fifteen years older than me approaches us. Of everyone else I've pulled in from alternate timelines, he's the least like me. His face is leathery and sun-scorched. He's completely bald, but more muscular than any of the others. A deep scar runs across his right eye, and he has a gaff hook where his left hand used to be.

"Eva," he says in a gravelly, tired voice. "Haven't seen you since...well right around now, I guess."

"Rosey?" Eva almost goes cross-eyed as she views my alternate future self. She blinks and glances between us both. "Rosey, what's the point of all this?"

"51, do you mind going over where you come from?" I ask.

"I've been through a decade of nuclear annihilation, ladies." He steps between me and our guests, standing as tall as he can against Eva's Amazonian stature. "Everything Roosevelt 37 told you has already come to pass for me. The other supers did take him out, but only after Masters City and most of the United States got turned into a sea of glass."

"Thank you," I say.

51 nods curtly and heads back to work.

"How do you know this is the right way to go?" Mei asks. "I mean, even if Mr. 51 there is right, doesn't that mean it's already predetermined?"

"If predestination existed, I would destroy this universe and rewrite it so it didn't," I say. "I brought 51 back with me because he happens to come from a future that's so bad he's willing to give up his own existence to avert it. No matter how much traveling I've done, there's one single constant I found in every future: Paradigm dies in the good futures, or he tears the world apart in the bad ones."

"Are you sure you're not biased?" Mei asks. "I mean, what counts as a good future for you?"

"That's a good question," Eva chimes in. "Rosey, exactly how many of these futures had you taking over the world?"

"Eva, you should know that the promise I made in prison still stands," I insist. "World domination doesn't interest me anymore—just world protection."

"You didn't answer my question," she says pointedly. "What was it you started to say back in my apartment about making a proclamation at City Hall?"

"Ah…" I could lie to her, but Eva will see through it. "That…is a temporary measure."

"It's a stupid measure, Rosey. You play that game, and the rest of the world is going to start throwing punches at you instead of Paradigm. If he's really the threat you make him out to be, you need to be able to prove it…and whatever timey-wimey ball you're playing with right now doesn't equal real proof."

"And how long are you willing to wait for proof?" I ask. "By my best bet, Paradigm's going to go nuclear in a matter of days."

"Then it's time to call in the authorities," she replies. "Throw yourself on the mercy of the court before you go too far and let other people get on the front lines. You're on this case as a consultant, not a detective. You get to help the cops—you don't get to bring the bad guys in yourself. Do what you have to in order to stop Paradigm, but do it from behind the scenes."

"Heh." Mei puts a hand over her mouth immediately, stifling a chuckle.

"What's so funny?" Eva asks.

"I just…I never realized you're the normal one here," Mei says. "I mean, I've got some phantom lady floating around in my brain, Dr. Pythagoras is…Dr. Pythagoras, and it's like you're speaking another language to both of us when you try to make things logical."

"Well, maybe you both need to listen to me," Eva snaps. "This is about common sense. Just because the world's going crazy doesn't mean we have to go crazy with it."

"It's hardly going crazy," I interject. "I'm going to save this world, whether its people want me to or not. You can argue about the methods until the bombs start falling, but I'm the only one with the means to stop Paradigm cold."

"How is this different from any of the other times you tried to take him down?" Eva asks.

I pause and consider the evidence. My plan seems foolproof, but don't they all?

"I have a good feeling this time," I say, wincing inwardly at the weak argument. "I also have the greatest assemblage of knowledge in the universe. To make the plan perfect, I only need an outsider perspective—somebody to keep me in check, to a certain degree. These Roosevelts have all my strengths, but they also have all my blind spots."

I turn to Mei first. If she's on board, it will be easier to convince Eva.

"What say you, Mei? Are you ready to help save the world?"

Mei winces like she's got a migraine. When she opens her eyes again, her face seems older and fatigued. "Miss Destiny might be willing to give you some leeway, but she's not driving right now. And I say this is a bad idea."

So much for Plan A. "A pity, but not unexpected." I nod to Roosevelt 25, who has been observing the conversation from the far corner of the cave. With a whirr and a crackle, Mei gets flung out of my lair, disappearing into thin air.

"Rosey, what did you just do?" Eva's seen this stuff a few times now, but she still acts like an amateur.

"Relax," I tell her. "She's back in your apartment, safe and sound." My voice grows softer. "But what about you? You see what I'm doing, don't you? You see how it's necessary?"

Her lips shake a little before she speaks. When she does talk, she does so slowly and sadly. "No. I can't do it like this."

"Says the woman who let Titan out of jail not too long ago."

She stiffens at that remark. "That was a lapse in judgment. I wish someone had been there to talk me out of it. And I'm trying to talk you out of this now. Look around you. You're worse off than you were before you went to prison. You've got an army of mad geniuses—"

"Don't call us mad," I warn.

"Sorry, but I don't know what other word to use. You're babbling about time travel and alternate futures and trying to commit premeditated murder. I have to call you mad, because the only other word I can think of is…evil."

I blink, then sigh. "It doesn't matter which word you use," I say. "Both are terms thrown out by people with small minds who don't understand true genius."

"Call me small-minded if you want," she says in an unyielding tone, "but remember I'm your lawyer. I advise you to stop this now. There are some things even I can't defend."

"Okay, that's your advice as my lawyer. What about your advice as my friend?"

She pauses, breathes in, and saus, "I'm not really sure I can consider myself your friend, Rosey."

I feel an acidic tang in my mouth and take a step backward. I don't have a retort. I don't have an emotion for this.

For one sickening split-second, I almost give in. I feel my shoulder shrug a quarter-inch as part of me gets ready to give up. After all, Eva's the wise one. But then I glance around the cavern, at the dozens of versions of me and at work I have devoted multiple lifetimes to complete. I can't give this up now. My calculations are perfect; I can't be wrong.

"Of course not," I say, conscious of how long the awkward pause between us lasted. "Everything between us was always strictly professional."

I nod to 25. Having not even met Eva yet, he thinks nothing of teleporting her out of my lair.

I look with dead eyes and a numb brain at the spot where she stood.

"Are you okay?" 25 asks.

Don't get sad, kid. Get angry.

"You should know," I tell my younger self. "Everything's going according to plan."

#22: THE BRAVE AND THE BOLD

I had one job, and I blew it. In the process, I might have broken the world.

I violated almost every ethical rule of my profession in order to set Rosey free, convinced that I knew better than everybody else. I deluded myself into thinking his time in prison had changed him. But now that he's got some new toys and a pocket full of excuses, he's worse than ever.

Then again, maybe it would be best for the bad guy to win this time.

Rosey didn't start this fire—that's on Paradigm. There could be a million different explanations for his behavior, from mind control to an alien doppelganger. The world doesn't care what those explanations might be. They're ready to drag the former American icon through the mud if it makes them feel safer. They might even turn to Rosey to save them. They might even be right.

There's no winning this time. We all get to choose between a vengeful nuclear-powered god and a supergenius with a Napoleon complex. And when the dust settles and the winner gets to write the history, it's all going to boil down to being my fault.

I come to realize that I'm laying down on my sofa, apparently having fallen backwards onto it the moment I landed back in my apartment. My face is blank and wooden, my eyes staring at nothing as I consider my doomed future.

Slowly, I become aware that Mei is shaking me.

"Eva?" she asks, desperately. "Come on, Eva. What's the plan?"

I look at her, but don't really see her. My sight stays locked a mile away, on a doom I created. "Why would I have a plan?"

"Because the whole world's about to fall apart! I have a date this weekend and I'm not about to let those two guys screw it up!"

"You should change the location of your date to a bomb shelter, then." I push her hands away and stand up. "There's not a lot I can do to stop Paradigm or Ros—" I clear my throat. "—or Pythagoras. Not all of us have magical superpowers."

Mei nods, her lips forming an almost invisible line on her round face. "And even those of us who do have them can't do a lot right now. I know. But the alternative is sitting around and doing nothing, and we can't do that can we? I mean, why go through all that trouble trying to rehabilitate Doc Pythagoras if you're just going to walk away when he falls of the wagon?"

"Falls off—?" I furrow my brow and straighten my posture. "This isn't an addiction he's trying to kick. We're talking about a guy who's been out of jail for less than a week and he's already plotting to take over the world."

My eyes drift away from Mei and stare intently at the blank television screen. Then again, maybe it is an addiction—just not a physical one. Maybe I should have pushed for an insanity plea after all.

And if it is mental illness, where does that leave us? A nuclear man who has grown so paranoid that he lashes out at the people he's sworn to protect and a mad genius who thinks the only way to fix this world is to conquer it. Both men need a padded cell and antipsychotics.

I brush the dust off my clothing. "I don't know where exactly we can go, but this looks like a job for—"

"For us," Mei interrupts. "But we need more firepower, first."

"Oh?" I ask. "Do you have a plan, then?"

"Well," she says slowly, "it looks like I'd better think of one, huh?

MEDDLING HEROES

The League of Liberty used to have a satellite base in orbit around Earth. That became an international space station after Rosey broke the League up, and secret superhero storage has never been the same. Instead of an orbiting satellite or a lair at the bottom of an ocean, Mei brings me to a run-down slum filled with boarded-up buildings and one out-of-business coffee shop.

Taking the entire ramshackle block in with one long glance, I notice things aren't quite what they seem.

"There's no garbage here," I say. "No bums, no kids looking to break in and see what sort of fun they can have in one of these abandoned buildings. It's like we're standing in a museum exhibit instead of an actual part of the city."

"You should tell that to her," Mei says. "She thinks her illusions are perfect, and she doesn't take criticism well."

"She's probably not in much of a position to snark back to me right now," I comment.

"I guess we'll find out." Mei stops walking at the barricaded front door of the coffee shop and closes her eyes. "She's the one who cast the illusion, so she's the one who needs to dispel it."

I put a hand on Mei's shoulder. "What happens to you if something happens to her?"

Mei shudders, sighs, and opens one eye. "I don't know...Mhasaz."

I let go of her shoulder as soon as she utters the first syllable of her magic word. When the smoke clears, Miss Destiny stands before me once again, though only as a shell of her former self.

The bruises have had time to darken now. There aren't too many on her face, but her costume is revealing enough to show a dozen or so purple splotches, cuts, and abrasions. She moves with a limp and can barely lift her right arm. She doesn't say anything when she materializes—just gives me a sidelong glance as though she's disgusted to be seen this vulnerable. Then she staggers toward the building and makes a few clumsy arcane gestures.

A purple haze rises off the buildings as though reality was melting away. The façade of a ruined coffee shop disappears, replaced with what I assume is the reality behind the magic—a squat black building with no windows and a pair of sliding steel doors serving as the only visible entrance.

Miss Destiny places a hand on one side of the building and says a single word. With a whoosh, the doors open and the building allows us to enter. I hustle in after her, and the doors close immediately behind me.

The interior looks bigger on the inside than it does on the outside—it's easily the size of an airplane hangar, with dozens of locked doors along each wall. White neon lights flicker, providing the illumination we need. Strange circuitry lines the floor in a pattern I don't recognize.

I notice a high-pitched humming that I didn't hear before. Miss Destiny limps to a control panel on the wall and punches a six-digit code into the console. In a moment, the hum goes away.

"A burglar alarm?" I ask. "I would've guessed you protected this place with some mystic runes or something."

"The combination of magic and technology is one of the defenses." Her voice sounds like she swallowed half the pavement that Paradigm knocked her into. "Some people can bypass magical wards, some people can hack security systems. Very few individuals can do both."

I raise an eyebrow. "Are you one of those individuals?"

"Not usually. Mei lends me...certain skills I do not normally possess. And I return the favor on occasion."

"What is this place, other than a high-tech storage locker?"

"It used to be a training facility." She presses a toe against one of the circuit patterns on the floor, then frowns when nothing happens. "It was a place where the League of Liberty could simulate the dangers we might run into in the field, but it seems to have fallen into disrepair."

"You guys gave up a lot of resources, all because Pythagoras messed with your brains that one time."

"You are speaking about a group of vigilantes who wear masks and keep their identities secret even from the ones they love." She sighs. "There were always trust issues. Dr. Pythagoras merely exacerbated them."

What else did Rosey exacerbate, I wonder? Was Paradigm always a bomb waiting to go off, or did Rosey light the fuse?

"I assume you know why we're here?" I ask.

She nods. "I must warn both you and Mei—getting between Paradigm and Dr. Pythagoras at this point is a path that can only end in death, no matter how prepared you think you are."

"But you're going along with the plan anyway," I note.

Her nearly-invisible pupils dilate slightly, making her look almost human for a moment. "Yes. I am."

I could drive a medium-sized sedan through the northernmost door. As Miss Destiny moves toward it, I notice it's the only door in this facility that isn't covered with a layer of dust.

My wounded companion first waves her arms to dispel a magical ward, then types something into the keypad on the wall. With a creak and a groan, the door slides open.

Rosey's prototype battle suit stands inside, the dents hammered out and the chrome polished. When Mei described it to me, it sounded like a beat up piece of junk. It looks like somebody's turned it into a reclamation project.

"Who else knows this thing's here?" I ask.

"Only Invisible Man and myself."

"Does it work?"

"Yes. Dr. Pythagoras himself tested it in his underground lair."

"Good," I say. "We have the tools. Now we just need a plan."

"In which case, it would help to know who our true enemy is," she replies. "Are we fighting Paradigm or Pythagoras?"

I take a moment to contemplate the question. "Maybe both. But it won't be easy. This thing's just a prototype. And the real suit didn't stop Paradigm, either."

"We can add it its power. My magical prowess may give us an edge that Pythagoras never possessed."

I turn away from the battle suit to make a show of sizing up the battered enchantress. "You're not exactly inspiring confidence in a battle right now."

"I will heal," she says through gritted teeth.

"Pythagoras said something about an announcement at City Hall. If he does the supervillain thing in front of them, that'll bring Paradigm out. If those two throw down in a populated area and Pythagoras plans on fighting to the finish, our best bet might be to focus on saving lives until it's all over."

"No," she said determinedly. "Our best option is to attack them both while they are distracted with each other. It is the only time we will have an advantage."

I curl my lip in disgust. "You're supposed to be a superhero. Doesn't avoiding collateral damage mean something to you?"

"I am a force of justice. Both individuals represent a threat to millions. More lives will be saved if we act swiftly and eliminate the danger while we can, regardless of other costs."

"You're treating people's lives like they're part of a ledger," I say. "That's not justice, that's an algebra equation."

"Need I remind you that your form of justice led us to this situation to begin with?"

I swallow my words with that one. I could admit that none of my actions in that case were just, but it seems like a moot point right now. Even debating the potential deaths of thousands, I don't seem to have the moral high ground.

"There's one more option," comes another voice. We both jump and then turn around as the air behind us fills with an electric crackle. A familiar man in a cape and cowl appears.

"It would've been nice for you to have joined us earlier, Captain Tomorrow," I hiss.

"I'm here now," he retorts. "And I'm here to tell you how the three of us are going to save the future…by doing nothing at all."

#23: BEYOND INFINITY

After you tinker with the fabric of space and time, you need to make sure to put all your temporal toys back in the right place.

One by one the alternate versions of me pop out of existence, each disappearing in a flash and rocketing through the fourth dimension to the time they came from. All they leave behind are the inventions which I will use to save the world. That, and the memories.

I remember things I didn't before. Singular moments in my past now play out in dozens of different ways when I recall them. My mind has become a muddle of temporal paradoxes and situations impossible for a normal mortal to comprehend.

Not so long ago, I tried to avoid this specific thing. I saw myself as an addict who needed to kick his habit. I spent five years detoxing in jail, pondering escape plans but going through with none of them. Those thoughts seem foreign to me now.

This is me. My lifestyle isn't a drug or a psychological crutch. I know how to kill Paradigm, and I almost quit when I was on the cusp of that realization.

Now I can see every angle, every possible result based on my actions from this point forward. I have double, triple, quadruple vision. So many different futures before me, and I can see them all.

Time has become meaningless to me. So I disappear, too.

The date of the first atomic bomb test. A German spy on the science staff, determined to stop America's progress toward victory. An enlisted man at the base found him out. A scuffle, a run. Somehow, they wound up on the testing field during the fateful countdown.

A gunshot. The spy crumples. But the enlisted man can't get back to the bunker in time.

A scientist rushes to save him. In his panic, he never notified the others to stop the countdown. Or maybe he didn't forget. Maybe he wanted to die.

In frenzied desperation, the scientist throws himself on top of the soldier, shielding him with his body. A futile gesture, yet one that somehow works against all odds.

A flash of nuclear fire, and a monster is born. But only I know the truth. Only I know that two monsters were created that day.

Click!
Click! Click!
Clickclickclickclick!

The Geiger counter speeds up as a man puts a gun to his head in a darkened room. Then, with a flash, the lights come on. The man lowers the gun and the Geiger counter slows down.

"You don't want to do that, Dr. Krenzler," I say.

He puts the weapon down on the coffee table with the same embarrassed expression a teenager dons when caught masturbating.

He's too preoccupied to notice that my fashion sense doesn't come from this generation—or any generation he's been a part of. I'm slumming it right now, wearing a pair of black denim pants and a collared shirt with the sleeves rolled up. Not even a decent lab coat to properly punctuate my genius.

"You've noticed the Geiger counter picks up the closer you get to killing yourself," I tell him. "The doctors couldn't find anything wrong in all their weeks of studying you, but you know there's something there."

His pupils contract, then dilate. I notice a smell on the air, permeating the small sitting room. Whiskey.

"Who the devil are you?" he asks, finally gaining some awareness of his surroundings.

"An admirer of yours. You've done great work, Doctor."

He snorts and rolls his eyes. The gun comes back up. The Geiger counter clicks again. His hand shakes in hesitation, but the barrel stays leveled at his head.

I glance around the room. His study has a rustic look to it, albeit cluttered with textbooks and manuscripts haphazardly strewn across most of the furniture. He took the trouble to light the fireplace and pull an overstuffed chair close to it before unpacking the gun. He gave himself every chance to die peacefully.

He growls. Before he has a chance to hesitate again, he places the barrel against the side of his head and pulls the trigger.

Click!

The Geiger ticks once more and then goes silent. Dr. Krenzler opens his eyes, not even realizing he had closed them. The gun is empty—has been since before he got here. I pull a single bullet out of my pocket and hold it at eye level.

"Why are you here?" he asks sullenly.

"Because I'm a hero," I reply matter-of-factly. "I'm going to save you."

"If you think my life is worth saving, you must really be the Devil."

"You suffer from severe bipolar disorder," I explain. "What people in your time call manic-depressive psychosis. You've spent your entire adult life exposing yourself to a cocktail of strange radiations that have changed your biological makeup. That bomb should have vaporized you and that soldier alike, but something in your cellular structure kept that from happening. Instead, it changed you both. There's no helping the soldier—his fate is already sealed. You, however, will remain yourself until the moment you fire that gun. The trauma won't kill you, but it will awaken the part of you that wants to live more than anything—that primal beast in us all that will do anything for survival." I let the bullet drop from one hand into the other. "He's quite admirable, in his own way."

"I've got to do this," Dr. Krenzler says. "If I don't—"

"Your work on the Manhattan Project is now a matter of record, Doctor. Even if you drop out now, the rest of the team will build on your research. The bomb is nearly complete."

"All the more reason for me to die and face my punishment, then."

I smirk. I come out of nowhere and start spouting gibberish from the future, and he just keeps talking about killing himself. He must think I'm some sort of hallucination. Or maybe he's taken the extremely limited evidence at his disposal and figured out the truth—there is a reason I admire him so, after all.

I walk to the fireplace and set the bullet on the mantle. "It's not the person who builds the bomb who needs to feel guilty, Dr. Krenzler. It's the people who can't think of a better solution but to set it off."

Then, in a flash, I'm gone.

With a few twists of wire and the tap of a button, the security cameras go blank. Well, not truly blank—just set to play old footage on a loop for a few minutes. Nobody monitoring the prison cell will notice a thing, and Roosevelt Pythagoras has all the time in the world to escape, should he so choose.

Not that he wants to, of course. I could have done this any time over the past few years but I chose to remain in jail, letting those fools think I was powerless.

I rap my knuckles on the bars. The other-me in the prison cell remains sitting in a meditative pose on his cot. He opens one eye and raises an eyebrow.

"Surprised?" I ask.

"Not very," last year's Roosevelt replies. "But I can't say I expected to see myself on the other side of those bars anytime soon." His pupils shift rapidly over my visage, putting together the evidence in a matter of seconds...still so much slower than I am now. "Time travel, then?"

"Indeed." I step back, cross my arms, and frown. "I pulled past versions of us from every other era in my life in order to complete my master plan, but I left you sitting in jail. Didn't even give you a chance to stretch your legs."

He seems nonplussed by this. "And why not me?"

And now, the hardest thing for me to admit. "I have no idea."

He shifts on his cot and leans back, bracing himself against the wall. "So why are you back here now? If you're from my future, what does this 'master plan' hold?"

I tilt my head and give a half-smile. "One guess."

He shakes his head. "No. We're not doing that anymore. That's why I'm on vacation in here."

I feel my jaw muscles clench. "Vacation? Did I ever really think of it that way?"

"It's better than taking yet another super-strong fist to the side of the head."

I grimace. "That can't be why I decided to stay here."

"Why not?"

"You tell me. Are you really okay with the idea that you're using this place as a hiding hole? Are you really going to admit defeat against Paradigm?"

His eyes widen and he starts to say something, but then clamps his jaw tightly shut. After a moment of silence, he finally responds. "And yet look at you. We get out of prison and then...what? We go right back to the same person we've always been."

"But I'm going to win this time."

"Then why are you here talking to me?" he asks.

"I still need somebody to check my work," I admit. "It wasn't so long ago that I had a different perspective on life. And I need that perspective if I'm going to avoid all the old mistakes. I'm going to show you the facts, get your feedback, and then leave you wondering if this was all a dream inspired by some bad prison meatloaf."

He stares straight ahead in silence, looking at me but also looking through me.

"This isn't a grudge anymore," I continue. "This is a matter of survival—of myself and of the human race. Will you help me become the hero we were always meant to be?"

After a long moment, he smiles. Then he nods.

I glance at the security cameras. Still disabled, but they won't remain that way for long. Then again, time doesn't really matter to me anymore.

Smoke chokes the sky. Buildings lie in ruin. The acrid smell of burning plastic reaches my nose. The pavement still sizzles from the recent cataclysm. I step over broken glass and charred bodies, my right hand holding a sleek black gun with composite plastic casing that seems to absorb the light around it.

I'm in a future that will never come to pass. In a way, this isn't really happening.

I find him simply by tracing the destruction back to its source. When I come upon him, he sits with his back turned to me in a crater where a skyscraper used to be—waiting like a spider at the center of a web of carnage.

"You..." Paradigm says as I climb into the crater and approach him. "I killed you."

"Did you now?" I ask.

He stands up and turns around. The costume's the same, but the mask is gone. His blond hair is streaked with grey. Wrinkles line his face, although they're more from fatigue than age. "I could kill you again."

"You're probably right," I reply matter-of-factly. "Even aged as you are, your super speed gives you the chance to break my fingers before I pull this trigger. But I don't think that matters to you. Not now."

He clenches his fist and lunges forward. My eyes only see a red and blue blur. Then he's within arm's reach, poised to knock my head clean off.

But he doesn't.

His fist trembles. The chiseled muscles in his arm quiver. Then he drops his hands to his sides and heaves a sigh.

"I didn't want it to be like this," he says. "But they wouldn't let it stop. First they loved me, then they feared me. Then…" he gestures toward the ruins of Masters City. "They tried to kill me. I had to fight back. They didn't give me any choice. They didn't realize their bombs and robots and tanks couldn't stop me." His eyes narrow and he looks at the gun in my hand. "Just like you never realized how useless all your gadgets and guns were."

"Oh, I always realized that." I keep the gun pointed away from him while I talk. "Think of it…I invented machines which could pull planets out of their orbit, control minds, and protect a normal person from a ground-zero nuclear blast. Do you have any idea how infuriating it was to have all that knowledge at my disposal and still be incapable of finding a weakness in you?"

"Maybe you should have given up," he says. "Your mind could have fixed the world, but you were too small to see that."

I know he hears the sound of my teeth grinding. I know he senses my muscles twitch as I almost put my finger on the trigger. He can stop me before I even aim my weapon. Even still, it takes all my strength to keep from firing blindly at him.

"Let me ask you something." I wave my free hand toward the landscape, taking in the blackened skies and decaying bodies of Masters City in one grand sweep. "What good is the cure for cancer now?"

He gazes at the emptiness around us. Miles upon miles of fire and pain and death. All caused by one thing that, despite all its power, seems so very small: him.

I give a dry, mirthless laugh at his stunned silence. "You know what the saddest part of our eternal struggle is?" I ask. "You almost changed me. I almost gave up in that prison cell. I had written off killing you as a lost cause and decided to put my effort into other projects that I thought could change the world. But you know what set me straight again? You tried to kill me."

"You were looking for an excuse," he says.

"And you gave me one," I retort. "You proved yourself to be the threat I always knew you were."

He grabs a piece of rubble off the ground and crushes it to dust in his fist. It seems to come from legitimate frustration rather than a desire to intimidate me. "It wasn't like that. You…they…they fired the first shot. I had to defend myself."

"Good job," I say dryly. "Now there's nobody left to threaten you."

"They never realized…I wanted to make the world better."

The lines of his face multiply and fold over each other as something inside him starts to break. I may have pushed him too far, but there's never going to be a better time to make my pitch.

"I can't—" I stop and correct myself. "I *won't* fix the events that turned us into enemies. But I can still stop this future from happening. I can guarantee the world will remember you as a hero. I just need your cooperation."

"How?"

I raise the gun. "I need a test subject."

Something blazes behind his eyes. For a moment I think he's going to kill me. Then the fire goes out. He nods and takes three steps backward, spreading his arms wide and closing his eyes.

"I still don't know if I can trust you," he says.

"Understandable." I take aim with the gun. "But believe me—this time, you definitely can."

I pull the trigger.

#24: FLASHPOINT

I have blood on my hands. No, not my hands—the metallic fingers of this suit I'm wearing.

My head aches. I can barely see through blurred vision. I think I might have a concussion.

What am I doing in this suit? And whose blood do I see?

The heads-up display in my helmet shows me a picture of the outside world. Mei on her hands and knees, retching. A body lies in front of her. The cowl looks familiar.

The corpse crackles with electricity, then ignites in a brilliant blue flash. It disappears, hurtling back in time.

Rosey didn't kill Captain Tomorrow. Neither did Paradigm. I did.

My brain does its best to repair the damage of the last few minutes. Memories rush back to me, filling in the out-of-order jumble that sense can recall but which my mind hasn't filed in the correct order yet. Is this what it was like for Rosey when he first took Captain Tomorrow's technology? Did he only know the end result and then have to piece things back together to figure out how it all happened?

"We stay out of it." Captain Tomorrow's voice comes echoing to me out of a past that isn't past. "Let Pythagoras play his hand. Believe it or not, he's our best chance of saving the world."

"That's ludicrous," I say. "You really want to see two people who have gone over the edge take each other on in front of millions of innocent people? I thought you fancied yourself a hero."

"So says the woman who lied in court in order to free a criminal," he throws back at me coolly.

I feel my face go red. "I fell off the slippery slope. I'm trying to climb back up, but you're apparently here to push me down again."

"Captain Tomorrow," Miss Destiny says. "Miss Corson will answer for her deeds in time. Whatever sins Paradigm has committed in recent days will be dealt with. But the clear and present danger is Dr. Pythagoras. His crimes, past and present, must be answered for. That you gave him your quantum technology without consulting—"

"Consulting whom?" Captain Tomorrow's voice grows hard and cold. "You started us down this path when you decided you could control him just by watching. It's not surprising that he ran off your leash."

"He did so thanks in no small part to your own meddling, Captain," Miss Destiny retorts.

"I meddled because I see things you can't." He taps the side of his cowl, and strange lights play across the lenses that cover his eyes. "It was just a matter of time before Paradigm started to crack. We held him back and kept him in check as long as we could, but now it's time to put him down. Pythagoras has always been right there, one punch or laser blast away from finishing the job. Now he has the weapon he needs to win. Do the right thing and stay out of this until it's done."

"I believe you are being short-sighted," Miss Destiny says. "I can still reason with Paradigm. Dr. Pythagoras, on the other hand—"

"If you're so sure he'll listen to reason, why did you hide this suit away?" Captain Tomorrow asks. "And if Pythagoras is such a danger, why did you spend so much time playing his games? Without your support he wouldn't have come across this case. He might not even have gotten out of jail in the first place."

"My reasons are my own," Miss Destiny retorts, "as are my contingency plans. But I assure you I have only justice in mind."

Captain Tomorrow shakes his head. "Ridiculous. You knew he was a snake, and you still let him bite you. But instead of learning your lesson, now you're letting an even bigger snake get within striking distance."

"If Pythagoras takes out Paradigm, what then?" I ask. "He'll be right there in position to finally realize all his megalomaniacal goals. Do you think he's just going to walk away from all that?"

"Pythagoras can be stopped," Captain Tomorrow responds. "I've analyzed this from every possible angle in every possible future."

"Was that before or after you gave him the ability to travel through time?" I snap.

Captain Tomorrow freezes. His jaw goes slack. I start laughing. It's all I can do.

"I can't believe this," I say with a cackle. "You people…you fly through the air acting like you're the perfect paragons of justice, but you're really just a bunch of muscle-bound idiots who fell backwards into superpowers. At least police officers get some real training. Now you've gone and given reality-warping powers to somebody who actually earned his place in life, a guy whose IQ is already off the charts and who can now manipulate time itself, and you think can contain him?"

"Shut up!" Captain Tomorrow barks, his face reddening. "I know what I'm doing!"

"No you don't." I take a step toward him, ready to push right by him if I need to. "Now…I'm going to get into that suit and do my best to stop things from getting even more botched up. Lord knows I've 'earned' the chance to play hero about as much as you have."

Captain Tomorrow draws himself up to his full height, puffing out his chest like we're playing some weird game of chicken. "Like it or not, you're not going anywhere."

Children. All these years, I've been dealing with children playing games in their pajamas.

"Get out of my way," I command.

Then I make a mistake. I put my hand on his chest and give him a shove. I just want to get by him so I can get to the one hope I have left to salvage this situation. But that's all it takes to irk him into action.

He starts with a simple judo throw. Grabbing my arm, he turns slightly and lets my momentum drive me off balance. I go over his shoulder and then hit the ground in the blink of an eye. The impact of my body hitting concrete leaves me winded and dizzy.

"Don't make me go any further than that, Miss Corson."

But he's already opened Pandora's box.

I've always refused to be a victim. I tolerate the male-dominated courtroom always eyeing my figure and giving me a harder time because of my gender. I endure that because I know I also threaten them. I'm a capable woman who has never been a damsel in distress. I've spent a lifetime maintaining my physique, my demeanor, and my reputation. By putting a slight dent in that armor, Captain Tomorrow has just threatened everything I hold dear.

I spring to my feet and lash out, kicking at the Captain's knees. But he's gone in the blink of an eye. Then he's behind me, driving an elbow sharply into the middle of my back and knocking me to the ground again.

"I'm a veteran time traveler, Miss Corson," he says as I stagger back to my feet. "I can see every move you're about to make. I've fought our fight already, in my head, in a million different ways. There's no way you can beat me."

"And yet you failed to predict this," Miss Destiny says.

She throws her arms wide and shouts a magic word. A burst of green lightning fills the air. It does nothing to me beyond making some of my split ends stand up, but Captain Tomorrow definitely feels it. He staggers like somebody just punched him in the gut.

"What did you do?" he hisses.

"I have altered the flow of time slightly," Miss Destiny responds regally. "My magical field has closed off any loopholes. While this spell lasts, I believe you will find time travel much more…difficult."

"You never told me you could do that," he growls.

"Apparently, she doesn't tell much of anything to anybody," I say. While he's distracted, I kick off my shoes and take a fighting stance. "Now, are you still going to stand in our way?"

My sudden surge of bravado doesn't last. Captain Tomorrow went toe-to-toe with some of the biggest baddies this world has to offer. I, on the other hand, only have about half a semester of tae kwon do under my belt.

He starts with a roundhouse kick and follows it up with a quick jab. I barely manage to block both attacks, but by taking the initiative he's already put me on the defensive.

I glance at Miss Destiny, hoping for some support, but she's rooted to the spot, trembling in exertion. Maintaining the spell in her weakened state seems to take everything she has. I have to turn things to my advantage before exhaustion catches up with her.

I haven't exactly had a great time of it in the past few days, but I decide I can still take a hit or two. Letting down my guard, I throw a punch and catch the superhero off-guard, grazing the side of his cowl. He grunts, but he's obviously had worse.

Three hard punches come in faster than I can anticipate, each striking in the same place just below my right temple. Colors flash across my field of vision. I find myself on the ground again before I even realize I went down.

By the time I stop seeing stars, Captain Tomorrow and Miss Destiny have been going at it for at least a few seconds. Gone are the theatrics and flashy powers that normally dominate these battles. With Captain Tomorrow's time travel disabled and Miss Destiny too exhausted to use any more spells, it's left up to punches, kicks, and headbutts. Both fighters have training in personal combat, but Miss Destiny has a split focus as she tries to maintain her concentration. When she drops, Captain Tomorrow will have us at his mercy, forcing us to sit by while Rosey throws everything I worked for away.

They pay no attention to me—I'm beneath their notice. Blood dripping out of one ear, vision blurry, thoughts scattered. All I see is the suit. At first I crawl toward it, then I manage to stagger to my feet. As Captain Tomorrow tosses Miss Destiny to the floor,

I climb inside. The armor locks over me almost instantly, cutting me off from the rest of the world. My skull aches as the light of a heads-up display gives me a real-time readout of what's going on outside. Wires wrap around my body, sensing every twitch of muscle and nerve. Within seconds, I become part of the battle suit.

Captain Tomorrow turns his attention away from Miss Destiny. She drops to the floor in exhaustion, but immediately puts trembling hands out again. With the last scraps of her strength, she keeps her opponent's time travel abilities bottled up, giving me the chance I need.

The Captain charges me. I cross my arms reflexively, and the battle suit follows my movements perfectly. His boot impacts the impervious shell of the armor with a loud clanking noise. Then, with a sweep of my forearm, I send him hurtling across the room.

I flick my wrist and a retractable blade springs out of the battle suit's forearm. The suit sways a bit, affected by my own lack of equilibrium. Still, I can only hope that the presence of a foot-long piece of razor-sharp steel serves as enough of a warning.

"You're not stopping us," I tell him.

"I have to," he responds. "Otherwise there won't be a tomorrow."

Miss Destiny whispers a word and then collapses. A spell? Maybe, though I doubt she managed to finish it. She doesn't transform back to Mei, and my heart skips a beat as I fear she might be dead. But before I can worry about her any further, the suit comes to life and starts moving with a mind of its own. The heads-up display crackles into static, then comes back into focus with a red targeting sight locked onto Captain Tomorrow's form.

"What are you doing?" I yell at the machine. "Stop!"

The suit moves faster than even Captain Tomorrow can react. I pull back with every ounce of my being, but the blade's already out and ready. The rest is too easy.

I don't even see the time between the stabs – just a repeat of the same motion again and again. One lung, then another. A third shot right to the center of his torso, and a fourth lower than that.

Four stabs. Four deadly wounds. Captain Tomorrow doesn't have time to react. He just stands there. Then he falls down.

My memory finally sorts itself out and starts playing things in their proper order. Mei's back and alive. She won't look at where the body had fallen, even though it's no longer there. Neither of us moves and neither of us speaks for a very long time.

Mei finally breaks the silence with a question. "We're in trouble, aren't we?"

The suit nods for me, reacting to the nearly imperceptible twitch of my neck muscles. The blade has retracted again. The metal limbs shake slightly, reflecting my own tense nerves.

Did I do that? I didn't consciously try to kill Captain Tomorrow, but I can't say I didn't want to hurt him. Did the suit respond to me, or is this some hidden program just waiting to be executed?

Rosey…did you make me a killer?

"Do we turn ourselves in?" Mei asks.

I know I should. I should get out of this suit right now and admit to everything I've done. But Rosey needs to be stopped, and I only have so many weapons at my disposal.

"We keep going," I say. "We can't change the past."

"Are you going to keep wearing that?"

The suit hums invitingly in my ear. It feels almost like a second skin already. My body tingles as the wiring reads my every thought and impulse.

"I need to," I say. "It's the only way we have left to save the future."

#25: AND THE WORLD WILL BE MINE

I didn't want to go down this road again, but then again world domination does have a certain appeal to it. There are only so many times people have looked at me with the respect I deserve, and almost all of those involved me holding some sort of death ray.

Paradigm has become the topic of the day. The mayor and the police commissioner called a press conference so they can lie and say they have the situation under control. Their caped marvel has thrown down the gauntlet, but these simpletons will convince themselves not to pick it up. As always, they need a real leader to show them the way.

I've interrupted the crème de la crème of public gatherings. I hijacked the communications at the World Peace Summit. I paralyzed the delegates of the United Nations with stun gas. I even dropped in on an OPEC meeting while piloting my battle suit. A simple press conference, even in a major metropolis following a devastating attack, barely rates for me. But it's still nationally televised and in a wide open public space, so it meets my needs. It's time to give the people what they want, one last time.

"We've had plenty of finger pointing and speculation," says the mayor, a pudgy, ruddy-faced man who practically hides behind his podium. "However, we also need to make sure that we properly evaluate any potential threat. I have been on the phone with the President, and we have experts in every field prepared to—"

I kill the power with the push of a button on a pocket-sized remote. The microphones cut out with a loud screech, the streets lamps burn out, and every building in a half-mile radius shuts down.

I rigged up a way to override Masters City's power grid in my spare time before breakfast today. It's an example of what I could have done years ago to the security system of the prison that held me—what I should have done, since it's obvious now that the world won't let me change.

I drop the remote on the ground, stomp it beneath my heel, and enact my latest plan.

"There's only one expert you need," I announce, my voice amplified by my hacked access to their speakers. "But I'm afraid I won't help you."

I enter from the back of the crowd, close enough that somebody might decide to be a hero and take a swing at me. I'm fully prepared to take that risk, because I've determined that I need a nice long walk to the podium. If I absolutely must rant, then I will rant on the move.

I'm in my power suit—not my battle suit, where I might have been more comfortable, but this is perhaps just as fitting. Aside from the sleek black gun on my hip, the only other difference between now and my court hearing a few days ago is that I'm not wearing tasseled shoes. Tassels, I have learned, are for chumps.

All eyes lock onto me. Security personnel have their hands on guns but seem afraid to draw them. This is as it should be.

"Ladies and gentlemen, your appointed hero is no longer here to save you. His mind is gone. He knows only paranoia and fear. Given time, he will destroy you and everything you hold dear. This is all as I have foreseen."

A look of realization dawns on hundreds of faces. Still nobody moves. They're like dogs hiding under their beds at the sound of thunder.

I continue my stroll toward the podium. "You branded me a madman. A maniac. You laughed in my face at my apparent failures, but now you all cower before me. And you do so with good reason."

Police officers take aim, a split-second away from firing. But they wield firearms designed to deal with common thugs and terrorists, not me. With practiced ease I press down on one of my cufflinks. The officers vanish in a flash. By the time they reappear, this will all be over.

A woman in the audience screams. Everybody else remains quiet. I reach the podium and dismiss the mayor. Click, flash, gone. My time now.

"You needn't worry about them," I say loudly. "In an hour, they'll be back right where they were, good as new. Then they'll have a chance to bow down before me like the rest of you."

Now comes the hard part—the lying. Luckily, Eva taught me how to lie convincingly. Otherwise, people might be able to see through my ruse.

"To answer your questions about Paradigm, his attack on Masters City was just a test run," I announce. "I wanted to see what my new weapon was capable of. Years ago I injected every member of the League of Liberty with mind-controlling nanomachines. The only one who seemed resistant at the time was Paradigm. Little did he know that it was all part of my master plan.

"Throughout my incarceration and subsequent release, the nanomachines have remained dormant in his body, adapting to his unique physiology," I continue, speaking with enough conviction to make my tale sound plausible. "Now they have given me a more permanent form of control. Your greatest hero has become my puppet. And this city—this planet—will meet my demands or I will deploy him like a bomb. What happened downtown was merely a sample of what I have the power to do. He doesn't have to stop until there's nothing but rubble and ash left of this pathetic, misguided civilization."

Verbal pandemonium erupts. "You maniac." "You'll never get away with this." "Somebody stop him."

I've heard it all before. They talk and talk, but they take no action.

I let them rage at me a bit before raising my hands and bellowing, "Silence!"

They obey like the good little lackeys they are.

"This press conference is now over. You came here to hear you leaders assess the threat to this city. As of this moment, Masters City is under martial law." I look at the press corps now, staring straight into their cameras. "This threat will spread to other cities unless my demands are met within the next twenty-four hours."

I take a deep breath. This is the least important part. I could demand pocket lint and they'd still resist on general principle. Since none of this part matters, I might as well go into full blown Christmas wish list mode.

"My terms are as follows," I say with relish. "The equivalent of one billion American dollars to be deposited into a private bank account. An immediate writ of military surrender acknowledging my unquestioned dominance of the United States of America. The cessation of all space exploration activities not personally authorized by me. The Lincoln Memorial altered to bear my likeness. Furthermore—"

More shouts of panic and outrage, but this time not directed at me. A pair of powerful hands claps together and creates a miniature sonic boom in the sky. Paradigm flies onto the scene and the assemblage of plebes finally scatters. These people just sat through a speech from a man laying the foundation of a bid at world domination, but it's their former hero who really scares them.

A crestfallen expression that no mask can cover up crosses Paradigm's face when he sees people reacting as they should. The hurt disappears in a moment, replaced by the rage that has clouded his mind as of late. His eyes glow as he looks at me, finding a target for his wrath.

"Finally," I say. "Now the fun begins."

The first punch knocks me several blocks away. That's one thing I've never quite been able to handle in a fight involving superstrength—the constant shifting of the battlefield.

I feel a pop in my back as I hit a brick wall. The mortar crumbles but holds, and I land ungracefully in a side street. Bystanders recognize me and start running before I can get back on my feet.

A white crackle of electricity comes off my hands as I dust off my power suit. My forcefield holds, and Paradigm hasn't even pushed it close to peak capacity.

"Cute," I say as I stand up again. "So much for the idea of nonlethal force, eh hero?"

The air ripples as he comes flying in. The fact that I still draw breath deepens his scowl—I should be nothing more than a greasy smear on a wall by now. Still, he flies deliberately enough that I can track his movements. He wants me to see him coming.

Such pride undeserved, Paradigm. Even in a paranoid rage, you're pathetically predictable.

I let him get close. A punch that could shatter my skull comes toward me. Taking a deep breath, I hold up my hand and...

Stop him.

With an impact that sounds like a bomb going off, his fist lands in the palm of my hand. My forcefield crackles as it strains to match his strength, but it holds. His arm trembles in exertion. Mine remains still.

"A little something I did with the unlimited time I had to prepare for this fight," I explain. "My forcefield feeds off the kinetic energy you create. Every punch you throw at me gets tossed right back at you."

I give his wrist a twist. Unfortunately, his bones don't break like I wanted them to. I just exerted enough energy to move an ocean liner, and all I gave him was a mild sprain. How can anything be this incalculable?

When he sees my face darken at the lack of impact I've made, he smiles. "All the prep time in the world, and you still can't beat me," he taunts. Then he smacks me with the back of his left hand, breaking my grip.

I fly back down the road, bouncing against the pavement like a stone skipping on water. A parked car stops me, and the alarm going off sounds like his laughter ringing in my head.

"Fine," I say, springing up as he comes in to land another hit. "We'll do this the other way."

I cross my arms and block his blow as he tries to collapse my chest cavity. Then I hit him with a haymaker, knocking him into the sky.

Sirens blare as emergency vehicles speed toward the scene. Camera crews won't be far behind. People on the sidewalks take cover in building entrances, but they don't stray too far away. They want to know whether Paradigm is their savior or destroyer. That means there are plenty of people within earshot as he comes back around.

"Well," I say, speaking as loudly as I can without yelling, "it seems you've managed to break free for a few moments. Enjoy it while you can, Paradigm. It's only a matter of time before the nanomachines adapt and take control again."

Poised to strike again, Paradigm pauses in confusion. "What are you talking about, Pythagoras? What game are you playing?"

"You should know better than anyone," I retort with glee. "I've had this planned from the moment I earned my freedom. Those little robotic bugs of mine have been dormant inside you for years, old chum. The sound of my voice is all it took to reactivate them. Once we spoke on that rooftop, you became a ticking time bomb. And now…kaboom."

He clutches his head as though something's trying to crawl out of his skull from the inside. "What? No you didn't! That can't be true."

"Can't it? You were already on edge, but you would never go berserk in the middle of a city like that. You needed a little push, and I was just the person to do it."

He floats lower now, trying to get a better read on me. I have to admit, the scheme certainly sounds plausible. Invent enough crazy stuff and people will believe you're capable of anything.

"Don't look so perplexed, Paradigm," I say. "You had to have suspected something was wrong. You've been feeling your age. You've been seeing the ants beneath you for what they are. You know you haven't been yourself, and you have me to thank for that."

He shakes slightly. Beads of sweat show up on his brow. It's an interesting psychosomatic reaction—he's fighting something that isn't really there.

Time for the grand finale. I grab the fender of a parked car and lift. The metal twists in my hands as I use up the last of the energy I borrowed from Paradigm.

"I turned the world against you." My voice rises to a wonderful melodramatic crescendo. "I convinced Captain Tomorrow to give me the power of time travel itself. And in a few moments, you will be back under my control. I. Am. *Invincible!*"

But there are always variables you can't account for. The car explodes in my hand. My ears ring, my vision fills with stars, and I stagger backward. I recover mere seconds later, and then I hear two simple words.

"Rosey. No."

A newcomer has arrived on the scene. My own battle suit, standing next to Paradigm. The first attack was nonlethal—a warning shot. But then the blades come out, and I see dried blood on them.

"Eva." I stand up and dust myself off. "I expected Captain Tomorrow first."

"Rosey, you're not as smart as you think you are."

I grin, running the numbers. "Well, we'll see about that."

#26: GREAT POWER

When he was in prison and still redeemable, Rosey told me about the long manic stints that could last for weeks. Night after night of constant work, coming up with new inventions most of us could never dream of. He claimed to have developed a purification system that would have eliminated all waterborne illness over the course of ten years had his board of directors approved mass production. During these periods, he'd sleep maybe two hours a week. The whole discussion left me wondering whether mad scientists would still be mad if they just took a nap once in a while.

Now I've rushed into a battle zone in downtown Masters City while wearing a powered armor suit designed to kill a superhero. And I didn't sleep at all last night. Does that make the same as Rosey?

Of course, my insomnia didn't come from a manic period of inventiveness. Instead, I just kept thinking about the person I killed yesterday.

I just wanted to redeem somebody. I wanted justice. Instead, I'm stuck with the knowledge that I made all this happen.

I still want justice. It's a nice concept, but I don't know if I would really recognize it if I saw it.

"Rosey, Captain Tomorrow isn't going to show. I killed him."

I hoped I wouldn't need anything more than those words. Just a simple verification that Rosey doesn't know everything. A reminder that he can be wrong, and that just having the highest test scores doesn't qualify him for ruler of the world. It almost gets through to him.

"Interesting," he murmurs. "All my calculations had assumed that today would be the day. But a completely accurate time of death is almost impossible to determine for a time traveler. If he died elsewhere, that means…"

My muscles relax. He's not too far gone. I can convince him to give himself up quietly before these new blades of mine do any more damage.

But I make mistakes, too, and I forgot about the unhinged demigod flying close by.

"Eva, look out!"

The warning comes from Mei. I told her not to follow me, but she's got just enough magic left to disobey me. She needn't worry about me, though. As always, Paradigm's gunning for Rosey.

In less than a millisecond, I find myself between Paradigm's fists and Rosey's head. The sound of his knuckles striking against the titanium shell of my armor rings like some sort of Armageddon bell. My feet dig into the streets, tearing up the pavement with metallic heels.

Now I know what faster than a speeding bullet really means. I just thought of where I needed to go, and the suit reacted. While I'm wired into this thing, I can even keep up with Paradigm.

But I don't want to. I must keep my mind on my goal, not on other possibilities.

"Listen to me, both of you! You can't keep doing this. You're going to kill everybody in this city!"

"He can't hear you," Rosey says. I can hear his rationality slip away, and it almost makes me sob. "He's too far gone. Any conscious thought he has left need to focus on fighting off my nanobots. The more he fights, the more they take over. Pretty soon, he'll go back to being my puppet."

"Shut. Up!" Paradigm rockets into the sky, then comes back down with a haymaker ready for Rosey. I try to get in the way again, but the aerial maneuvers I just learned a few hours ago can't compete with skills he's acquired over the course of decades. He dodges past me and throws a punch that could knock a person straight to the Earth's core. Rosey doesn't even get his hair mussed. Effortlessly, he catches Paradigm by the wrist and comes back with a punch that connects right with his squared jaw, sending him flying into the stratosphere. In an instant, he's nothing more than a crimson dot in the sky.

"Rosey," I ask, "what is all this? Why do you keep yammering on about nanobots and mind control?"

I don't even know if he hears me anymore. He just looks at me with those hyperactive mad scientist eyes of his and says, "You're going to want to duck."

A sonic boom causes a nearby fire hydrant to burst, but Paradigm's back in the fight even before the noise alerts me as to his presence. He grabs my shoulder, lifts me off the ground, and tosses me into a brick wall. Then goes for Rosey again.

Half of me wants to insult him for being stupid enough to keep punching when it's obvious that Rosey can reflect everything back at him. Then I realize that he learned a thing or two after all.

Instead of engaging Rosey directly, Paradigm uses his speed. He zips to and fro, keeping his opponent off-balance. He feints left, then pulls his punch at the last moment and darts twenty feet to the right. Before Rosey can track him, Paradigm has rocketed around behind him. Then he takes to the air and goes high. He still can't land a punch that hurts, but the mere fact that he's doing something unexpected gets Rosey worried. The smile disappears. For the first time in the fight, he reaches for his gun.

The sensors on my suit can't make out what the thing is. All I have to go on is my instinct, and I don't need a lot of that to figure out that it's the newest in the line of weapons that will fail to kill Paradigm. Both Paradigm and I see him put his finger on the trigger. As he fires, the gun lets off a hum that I can feel in my teeth.

The weapon shoots what I can only describe as black lightning. It looks impressive as hell—I can only imagine Rosey's disappointment when it misses by a mile.

Paradigm veers skyward at the last millisecond, traveling a hundred feet in the time it takes the gun to finish discharging.

"You wasted all that time on another broken toy, Pythagoras," he says with a laugh.

He's playing his own head games now. The laughter was meant to set his opponent off. Instead, Rosey just gets deathly silent as the cocky smile becomes a stone-faced look of determination. The crimson-clad crusader flexes his muscles and burns hot enough to melt concrete.

Even though it seems like Paradigm has caught Rosey flat-footed, I can see the wheels turning behind my former client's eyes. He's trying to calculate every single variable, from wind resistance to the twitch of Paradigm's super-powered muscles. In his mind, if he can get all the math just right, he can shoot Paradigm dead before he lands his next punch.

Poor Rosey…never learning to account for human inconsistency.

Maybe it's as simple as Paradigm shifting slightly to the left instead of the right. Maybe a butterfly flaps its wings on Broadway. Whatever the reason, Rosey's careful shot misses by a hair's width and his foe keeps rocketing straight ahead. Paradigm stops inches away, grabs Rosey's belt buckle, and crushes the circuitry powering the forcefield.

The device crackles and billows out an acrid smoke that smells like burned dog hair. Rosey's expression turns bleak as he realizes that he's lost again.

"Thank you for telling me how it works," Paradigm hisses through clenched teeth.

He snatches the gun out of Rosey's hand and breaks it in half. A crackle of black lightning bursts from the invention, striking each of us with thin arcs that tingle but do no obvious harm. Then Paradigm pulls his fist back slowly, ready to finish his nemesis off once and for all.

No—he's not pulling his fist back slowly. It only seems that way to me because of the enhanced senses given to me by the suit. And that's the flaw in Rosey's plan—he focused so much on being able to out-punch Paradigm that he didn't take his speed into account. So while Paradigm's fist flies toward Rosey's head must seem like an indescribable blur to him, it takes forever to me.

I lunge forward and haul Rosey safely out of the way before Paradigm can put a fist through his brain. The broken gun clatters uselessly to the ground. The crimson-clad psychopath swipes at open air, then looks at me and growls.

"I remember that suit," he says. "It didn't do very well against me."

He takes to the air, illuminated by flashes of black lightning that still linger around the battlefield. I return the charge as we fly toward each other at top speed. The resulting shockwave scatters emergency crews and nearby aircraft away like leaves in front of a gale. For once, I'm thankful I don't have Rosey's intellect—that way I can't contemplate the collateral damage.

His punches rattle against my torso like jackhammers. I land one good shot right on the bridge of his nose, but he definitely wins this round. By the time we disengage, his hair is ruffled and has a bit of blood on his upper lip. But he also has a large chunk of my armor in his hand, which he crushes into a fine powder.

I touch a hand against the exposed circuitry and torn metal on my chest. I can't win a fistfight against Paradigm. Nobody can. But I also don't have some macho need to prove that I can punch him out.

I focus on defensive maneuvers as he makes his next approach. I just dodge at first, and then lead him in a small circle. Then I pick up speed, and that circle becomes tighter. Pretty soon I'm moving faster than most eyes can see, creating a cyclone around Paradigm.

Warning lights flash in front of my eyes and klaxons blare in my ears as I redline the suit. Safety parameters are for people who have a backup plan. I need to win now.

Paradigm doesn't realize what's going on just yet, and that works to my advantage. He braces for another punch and doesn't figure out what I'm doing until he comes up short of breath. I've sucked the air right out of his lungs.

I close my eyes and do my best to tune out everything else but the thought of more speed. I can't hear anything beyond the rush of air my own vortex is creating. I must have already created a sonic boom—not that I'd hear it, considering the speed I'm traveling at. As fast as I'm going, I keep pushing myself faster, creating a vacuum at the center of the vortex.

Only when the suit starts to falter and slow do I open my eyes again. My skin blisters as the circuitry overheats. Paradigm's on his hands and knees, gasping for air. Blood oozes out of his ears.

I keep the pressure on. Rocketing downward, I hit him with all the power the suit has left. I hear the crunch of bone. Then I keep pounding until he stops trying to get up and the suit doesn't have enough energy left for me to even lift my arms.

And then, silence.

Everything seems suddenly quiet and calm. Even the sirens and shouts seem to be miles away, hidden beneath a high-pitched whine. I think I might have punctured my eardrums.

Any potential bystanders have fled by now. Rescue crews are setting up a perimeter, hoping to contain rather than confront. The only two people inside that perimeter are Rosey, kneeling and watching my actions in shock, and Mei, standing next to him like a bodyguard—or a cop about to make an arrest.

"You need to turn yourself in now, Rosey," I say.

I glance at Paradigm. He's alive. I can see him breathing. His arms and legs twitch, but I'm confident he'll stay down. Nobody can take a beating like that and keep going.

General Lucas can lock Paradigm in a holding cell. Rosey is destined for jail once again. And the hero of the day...is me.

#27: FOILED AGAIN

I mastered space travel in my teen years. I have nine PhDs. An IQ that cannot be measured by modern standards. Yet I am still an idiot.

Eva manhandled Paradigm in a suit she's barely familiar with. Only a lack of understanding regarding his recuperative powers keeps her from finishing him off. I've invented gadgets that allow me to stand toe to toe with gods, move planets out of their orbit, and send others hurtling through time, but none of it matters. Unlike Eva, I don't think well on my feet.

Fortunately, winning this fight was never my Plan A.

"You need to turn yourself in now, Rosey."

If she had asked me to do that at the beginning, I would have done it for her. At least that's what I want to believe. But now I'm too close to the end to leave the job unfinished.

I put my hands up. That move always buys me time because they never understand the depths of my contingencies. And as much as I adore Eva, right now she's a "They."

"I need you to listen to me very carefully," I say, and she does. She's so good at this, and yet so green at the same time. She doesn't realize the precious value of seconds. "You have me beaten. But you don't have him beaten."

She glances at Paradigm, but it's already too late. He has his second wind, and now he knows she's a serious threat. He springs back to his feet and has her in a grapple before she can even think about responding.

He goes about dismantling the armor, ripping it to shreds just like he did to my other suit five years ago. The force coming from his fists nearly knocks me off my feet. Each super-fast blow combines to sound like the eruption of a volcano. Eva tries to fight back, bless her, but she's completely unprepared for the renewed assault.

"Help her!" Mei cries, shoving me in the back.

"Why don't you help her?" I retort. "Summon Miss Destiny and save the day."

She locks her jaw tightly and stares angrily at her shoes.

"Don't worry," I mutter. "I've already done everything I can for her."

Having the breath literally ripped out of his lungs delayed Paradigm for less than 30 seconds, as I anticipated. Even as his mind has changed, his physical capabilities remain within established parameters.

I've had Paradigm at my mercy and on the verge of death four separate times—more than any other foe in his long and storied history. And while he escaped each one of those deathtraps, every failure left me with a little more data. The miseries of my past gave me all I needed to make sure that when I did get a shot, I made it count. But first, I had to do the impossible. I had to accept that I could never beat Paradigm on my own.

Black lightning reminiscent of my entropy ray seeps out of the cracks that Paradigm opens up in the armor. It surrounds Paradigm in an ominous crackling shroud of black lightning as he deals blow after devastating blow to Eva. The attack must terrify her, but I remind myself not to interfere yet. The modifications I made to the suit protect her as intended. After all, I know exactly how much pressure Paradigm can apply down to the last Pascal. The suit's sensors shut out the pain, even when he lands his best haymaker and cracks open the torso.

Under the armor, Eva still wears her suit and business skirt. The modifications I made to the neural network spared her from having to strip down to her underwear like I used to. Even in defeat, she won't lose her dignity.

That dignity keeps her in the fight longer than expected. She's too prideful to go down, even when all seems lost. Her grit and determination keep her standing even as pieces of the armor fall off her body. When Paradigm finally slows down to catch his breath, that spirit allows her to roll free from the wreckage and sprint toward Mei. She throws her body over her companion, trying to shield her from the certain doom to come. The gesture is touching in its futility—something I would never do for another human being.

"Feeling your age, old man?" I call, reminding Paradigm that I exist. I glance upon the flush of his face and the sweat on his brow with a satisfaction I once feared I would never feel.

Paradigm surveys the battlefield to find no other threats standing against him. Then he chooses to settle old scores and marches toward me.

Marches, not flies.

He punches me in the jaw, and his eyes bulge when he notices that my head remains on my shoulders.

"What…what's going on?" he gasps.

"This is what it feels like to be me," I explain. Then I punch him in the face.

The impact makes me wince. Even with all the time in the world to prepare, I still can't throw a proper punch unless I use a hydraulic fist. Nonetheless, the force and the shock of the situation knock him off his feet. He hits the ground for a change, and now I'm the one standing over him.

"This won't work, Pythagoras. This…argh!"

Now the pain begins. His insides have caught fire. Or, more accurately, the fire that provides him with his power is going out.

"I borrowed more than Captain Tomorrow's technology," I explain, indulging myself in the satisfaction of a monologue for just a moment. "I borrowed some of his tactics. How did he beat me last time? He jumped into the past and put a small but fatal flaw in my armor. I borrowed from his book…except this time the armor's flaw exposed you to the same type of energy I knew you'd dodge when fired from a gun. I would have liked my shot to be the thing that beat you, but I'll take what I can get."

He tries to stand up. I kick him in the stomach. When he hits the ground again, I press my heel against his chest.

"You've been dodging the laws of thermodynamics for years, Paradigm. Now it's catching up to you. From here on out, you get to learn what it feels like to be human again. Of course, there's a small chance you might just go into full meltdown mode and leave nothing but a smoking radioactive crater behind. Let's wait and see, shall we?"

He tries to grab my ankle, but I spring backward. He staggers to his feet and takes another swing, but I catch him in an arm lock before it connects. I shift in posture, and his own momentum carries him back to the ground.

"You always relied on your powers, while I—"

No. Stop talking now. It seems like you've won, but you haven't. You were never playing to win.

Nobody else sees the big picture right now. Nobody else knows the Armageddon that my actions have prevented. They see their hero lying helpless, and they see the world's greatest villain standing over him in victory. The police will move in to try to stop me at any moment. Maybe they'll give me a warning. Maybe they'll just shoot to kill.

This is all as I have foreseen. I gave them an out, a way to believe that everything Paradigm has done up to this point was part of some grand scheme of mine. If they're stupid enough to believe that, if they're really so desperate to remain blind, then I don't want their adoration. In a world where people beg for heroes to do everything for them, where they refuse to better themselves because they're afraid of failure, I'd rather be a villain.

"Pythagoras," Paradigm hisses. He tries to get up again, but stumbles. "This isn't—" But he doesn't finish the sentence. He lands face-down on the ground and loses consciousness.

I turn toward Eva and Mei. Then I put my hands on my head and drop to my knees.

"I surrender...for real this time."

The police are still minutes away from making the actual arrest. Eva walks toward me.

"I'm not going to defend you, Rosey," she says. "I quit."

"I know," I respond with remorse. "One of the curses of time travel is that I know which of my ideal futures will never come to pass."

"Before they take you, tell me something."

"Of course."

"The suit…when I killed Captain Tomorrow, it was like I didn't have any control over my actions. Did you do that? Did you turn me into a killer?"

I furrow my brow. I thought I was done with these unexpected variables. "No. I modified the suit knowing you would use it, but I never—"

"Mhasaz!"

Mei's magic word is quickly followed by another arcane syllable from Miss Destiny's lips. Eva stands up like she's just touched a live wire—she's heard this spell before. And then it all makes sense to me, but it's too late.

The wounded sorceress waves a hand, and I hear a clatter from behind me as the ruins of the battle suit come to life. I turn my head and see the blade that killed Captain Tomorrow hurtling toward me out of the corner of my eye. It's the only warning I get before my impending demise.

Powered by magic, the blade does only what it needs to do and nothing more. I don't even have time to give a rueful smile. Miss Destiny's magic always was a blind spot for me.

"No!" cries Eva. "What did you do?"

"Justice," is Miss Destiny's only answer.

My hands drop to my side. With my last reflex, I touch the black box in my pocket—yet I'm too late to use it as an escape plan like I intended. A blue field of quantum energy crackles around me, and I shift back in time just before I draw my last breath.

It looks like I've been foiled again.

#28: GREAT RESPONSIBILITY

After all the time travel, apocalyptic battles, and high-tech armor, a moment of peace and quiet scares me.

I give my statements and interviews. Then the damage control teams take over. Days later, it's just me sitting in my bedroom, staring at a wall, and contemplating my many aches and bruises.

I should be in spin mode. Salvaging my reputation wouldn't be very hard. With all his talk about mind-control and plans within plans, Rosey gave everybody a defense if they want to use it. No, your honor, it wasn't me who lied to the court, conspired with a convicted criminal, and drove an increasingly unstable superhero over the edge. It was all the doings of evil old Dr. Pythagoras. I was just an unwitting pawn.

But then, that would be the biggest lie of all, wouldn't it?

I acted just like Rosey, meticulously calculating everything in advance. But my plans were all based on a false assumption: the idea that I could redeem him.

I though he just needed to get out of that cell and use his genius to help society. But I didn't see the rest. I didn't see how easily Rosey would slide back into his old ways once he had the right excuse. I didn't see a superhero community that had grown paranoid over the years or a society that turned a blind eye as the world conspired against its own protectors. I didn't see a world that valued security over hope.

The sun sets, and I'm left sitting in the dark, staring straight ahead at nothing.

I didn't see.

A visitor arrives shortly after midnight. She doesn't use the door. I had dozed off a bit, but my consciousness snaps back once I smell the telltale scent of licorice and lightning.

"Eva," Miss Destiny says as she steps through a solid wall.

"You murdered him," I say, my mouth dry. "You turned Mei into a criminal."

"I said Mei was close to redemption. She was. The pursuit of justice sometimes requires that we get our hands dirty."

"What about when it's not your hands? That spell you cast during our fight against Captain Tomorrow—you took control of the suit. You used me as a puppet."

"Captain Tomorrow would have regained his full capabilities had I waited any longer. He would have won that fight and prevented us from intervening in the battle between Dr. Pythagoras and Paradigm."

"He thought Rosey would win without us. If that happened—"

"Then Dr. Pythagoras would not have been punished for his part in this disaster."

"Punished?! He had already surrendered! He was on his way back to jail!"

"And we saw how well that ended last time."

"Mei still blames herself for the death of her parents," I say. "Bonding with you was supposed to make up for that. It was supposed to give her a chance to pursue justice."

"There are many forms of justice, Eva," Miss Destiny says in a hollow voice. "My definition happens to be much older than most. Whatever good intentions he may have had, Dr. Pythagoras was responsible for the deaths of many. He earned his fate."

"So what about Paradigm?" I ask. "What makes knocking down a few skyscrapers forgivable? Why didn't you stab him in the back, too?"

Her nearly pupil-less eyes seem to darken. "His good deeds in the past have earned him a reprieve…for now."

"Did you just come in here to argue philosophy?"

"No. I came here to say goodbye. By stopping Pythagoras, the balance has been fulfilled. Mei's time as my host is finished."

"You can't make up for two people's deaths by killing another one," I hiss.

"In this case, you can." Lavender smoke begins to surround her, but thinner than normal. "Goodbye, Eva."

Her tall, statuesque form melts away, evaporating with the mist, and she once again becomes the innocent teenager I wanted to help. Mei staggers, and I spring to my feet to catch her.

"It had to happen this way, right?" Mei's face is ashen, her eyes searching.

I say nothing.

"We saved the day, didn't we?" she implores me.

"You're okay now," I say.

"I remember killing Dr. Pythagoras. Like, actually killing him. Do I…um, do I need a lawyer?"

"He was a supervillain in the middle of a rampage." The words feel odd on my tongue—like I'm discussing a historical figure rather than somebody I might have had a drink with. "Nobody's going to press any charges."

Mei presses the toes of her sneakers into my beige carpet. "If they did…if I was looking at a jail sentence, would you defend me like you did Dr. Pythagoras?"

I give her question the benefit of a moment of thought. Then I shake my head. "No, Mei. I'd do it right this time."

More time passes and I become increasingly disturbed about the lack of consequences. Instead of going to jail I become a celebrity, cameras in my face and reporters asking me how it felt to fly around in a power suit. I don't correct them by explaining that they should call it a battle suit.

For days I expect a summons or at least a professional warning from the Bar Association. I violated virtually every ethical code in existence to release Rosey from prison. But as far as anybody can see, Rosey mind-whammied me into doing his bidding, just like he did with Paradigm. Nobody tries to dig any deeper than that. They're all ready to accept the surface story because it's a convenient one to believe.

Once I've stopped answering my phone, the news media turns to Rosey's old classmates, board members at RP Industries, and anybody else who can provide them with a glimpse of the human behind the psycho. But very few people ask one of the most important questions of all: what happened to Paradigm?

Am I dreaming or am I awake? I may never know.

I hear the light drizzle of summer rain outside my bedroom window. There's no sound, no indication that somebody has broken in, but I find myself startled out of a sound sleep nonetheless. Drowsiness still dominating my brain, I check each corner of my bedroom. Standing near the door, as far away from my bed as possible, is a familiar form.

"Rosey?"

"Eva." Illuminated only by the ambient light radiating from a slumbering city, Rosey takes one step forward. He's wearing his power suit—the one he wore when I sprang him from prison, and the one he wore on the day he died.

"You know you're dead, right?" I ask.

"Maybe," he responds.

Maybe? Of course—he's got Captain Tomorrow syndrome. From his perspective, the moment of his death hasn't arrived yet.

"You're going to die," I correct myself. "If you fight Paradigm again, Miss Destiny will—"

"Eva, I know. That's already happened."

"What?" My sleepy brain tries to sort through the facts. Did he mess with the past to prevent his own death? If my past changed, what would it feel like? Would I even notice?

"I'm not from the past," he says. "I'm me, right now."

"How is that possible?"

He grins. "What if I told you there was a clone after all? What if I told you I teleported to a secret base where a robot servant resuscitated me? What if I told you I had a hidden mystical amulet that protected me from Miss Destiny's power?"

I pause a moment and consider each possibility in turn. "I'd believe any of those explanations," I say at last.

"Exactly. This world has infinite potential. How can I leave that behind?"

He straightens his tie, and that's the last thing I remember until I wake up in the morning. When I come to, I'm still in bed, undisturbed and under the covers. A search through my apartment reveals no sign that anybody else was there.

It had to be a dream, right?

Anybody who paid attention to Rosey's career would have noticed that he was acting out of character from the moment he arrived in front of City Hall. He liked to talk plenty after the fact, but when the job was on he clammed up, just in case. That was one of the only reasons I manage to set him free in the first place. If he had ranted and raved like that in the past, there wouldn't have been any reasonable doubt at all.

I know part of it has to have been his attempt to give me some plausible deniability. Whatever he had planned, he surely wanted me to get away free if things fell apart. But the biggest effect that Rosey's rant had was that it turned all of Paradigm's recent actions on their head. Instead of being a high-strung vigilante who finally went off the deep end, he became a victim of the devious Dr. Pythagoras. Instead of becoming the criminal Rosey saw him as, Paradigm might soar the skies again—if his powers ever return.

It won't take somebody with my skills to win this case. Anybody who's ever been through law school could sell reasonable doubt to a jury on this one. And if Paradigm's going to get pardoned for his crimes, it needs to be for the right reasons—not because Rosey pulled a fast one as part of some inscrutable master plan.

After a strong cup of coffee, a hot shower, and a merciful lack of additional dreams, hallucinations, or visits from dead supervillains, I hit the road. I rely on the GPS to guide me, although it seems like I could get there on instinct alone. It looks like a small silver trailer in the middle of the Great Plains, but there's a vault down there that could hold God Herself.

I park on the side of the road well away from the facility and start walking. The soldiers examine my briefcase for weapons and explosives, wave a security wand over me, and then escort me in to meet General Lucas.

Officially, Paradigm is being held for evaluation until they can make sure that whatever nanobots Rosey used have burned out of his system. But I know the facility's true purpose—or at least I think I do.

It was built by the late Solomon Krenzler, sometime after he won his second Nobel Prize. Nobody knows why the scientist built it or what kind of monster he intended it to hold. The one thing I do know for certain is that I get a stunningly vivid sense of déjà-vu once I enter the building.

"I can't tell you anything more than I already have," General Lucas says as the elevator brings us down to the bottom sub-basement.

"Nobody explained why they want him here?"

"Just precautions, as far as I know." He casts a glance toward the security camera watching us, then clears his throat. "Look, Eva," he says in a lower tone of voice, "you were right there when it all happened. If somebody like you or me wanted to cause that kind of chaos, it would take years of planning and at least a dozen different allies. This guy nearly blew up a city without breaking a sweat. Accident or not, it's past time to watch out."

"Our hero, huh?"

The elevator doors open. General Lucas waves me toward a door at the far end of the hall.

"Maybe," he says. "Maybe not anymore."

Beyond the door sits someone who fought the Nazis and survived at the heart of a nuclear explosion. He doesn't look anything like the man who showed up in my office just over a week ago. His uniform has been confiscated, replaced with a gray prison jumpsuit. He still has the bodybuilder physique, but it looks softer now. His blonde hair has become speckled with gray, and wrinkles have finally worked their way into his statuesque features.

"You'll pardon me if we don't shake hands," he says from behind the plate glass window. "Even if I wanted to, the machineguns mounted in the corner would open fire if I got too close to you." He holds up his hands. They tremble slightly. "Of course, that wouldn't be much of a problem up until just recently."

"You'll get used to it," I say. "Just like the rest of us."

"Maybe. Or maybe it won't last," he says. "I've lost my powers before, and they always came back."

"And what would you do if they did come back?" I inquire. "Make us all pay?"

He clenches his fist experimentally, then relaxes it. "What do you want, Miss Corson?"

I place my briefcase on my lap and snap it open. "I want the world to make sense," I say while rummaging through papers. "But barring that, I'll stick to what I know."

"Are you serving me with a lawsuit?"

"No." I remove a form from the case and place it in the sliding plastic tray the guards use to get him his meals. Then I set a felt-tipped pen inside and slide the tray through to his side of the cell.

He looks at the document like it's rancid meat. "You want to defend me?"

"I want to redeem you," I reply.

He glances back at the contract, then turns his gaze back toward me. Finally, he picks up the pen.

I swear I can almost hear theme music start to play.

ABOUT THE AUTHOR

Charlie Brooks is an award-winning author, avid comic book collector, husband, father, and lifelong Vermonter.

His accolades include the Chaffin Award for Fiction for his short story "Fantasy as you Like It" (published as Charlie Martin) and the New Millennium Writings Fiction Award for his tale "Eight-Bit Heaven." In addition to a wide array of magazine articles, short stories, and gaming products, his novels include the fantasy epic *Shadowslayers*, the dystopian sci-fi story *Reality Check*, and a pair of young adult fantasy novels: *Greystone Valley* and *Conquest of Greystone Valley*.

For a full listing of publications, awards, and musings, please visit www.ChBrooks.com.

Made in the USA
Middletown, DE
13 April 2023

28718130R00116